The Healers

The Healers

Kimo Armitage

A Latitude 20 Book

UNIVERSITY OF HAWAI'I PRESS
Honolulu

Fat Ulu, an educational nonprofit, contributed partial funding for this publication. Their mission is to bring literature into Hawai'i's communities.

21 20 19 18 17 16   6 5 4 3 2 1

Library of Congress Cataloging-in-Publication Data
Armitage, Kimo, author.
  The healers / by Kimo Armitage.
      pages cm
  "A Latitude 20 Book."
ISBN 978-0-8248-5645-8 (pbk. : alk. paper)
1. Healers—Hawaii—Juvenile fiction.   2. Hawaii—Juvenile fiction.   I. Title.
  PZ7.A729He 2016
  [Fic]—dc23

                                                                2015019375

Designed by Milenda Nan Ok Lee

Cover Art: DNA Memory by Maile Andrade

For Kaulalena, Wahinemaikai, and Pualani with aloha

The Healers

Great Was the Cousins' Love for Each Other

THEY DREAMED OF EACH OTHER while in their mothers' wombs. When their mothers would salt pork together in the kitchen, the children would kick. While their mothers were fervently praying together, the children would push inside their mothers. Soon, the mothers began to understand the nature of these cousins' great love for each other.

The mothers were not surprised when the children were born the same day.

One of the children did not survive. She died inside of the womb of her mother. At the exact time that she died, the other cousins kicked furiously and tore their placentas with their feet. And this is how the other two children were born.

Keola was born first, and Pua was born after him.

Pua and Keola were sad because of the loss of their cousin. They cried for six months without stopping. It was love that caused them to wail incessantly and caused their tears to dampen their cheeks.

The parents were frightened for their children. They took them to Hawaiian doctors, Japanese doctors, and to Chinese herbalists, but they were unable to find a cure.

The crying was loud, but the parents would use the noise to scare away rats that would come into the kitchen. They would also scare away wild pigs that came into their vegetable gardens.

One day the family decided to go to the beach. Before this, they had never taken the children to the beach because the family did not want the children to scare away the fish. But this day was especially hot and the family had already eaten.

As soon as Tutu placed the two children in the cool water, they stopped crying. They smiled. Then, they laughed. After that miraculous day, whenever the children would start to cry, the family went to the beach. The two children stopped crying and the family simply believed that the salt water had cleansed their grief.

The Wound without Blood

TUTU WANTED TO EAT BLOOD SEAWEED so she told Pua and Keola, "Children, let's go for a ride." They put away their tricycles and hopped into the backseat of the Mazda.

All they took with them was a single sack to carry the limu. They did not take anything to eat or anything to drink because Tutu was simply going to get some limu and they were going to return home.

As soon as they arrived at the beach, Tutu started to harvest blood limu from the reef bed, and the children went for a short swim. While the children were playing, a fish came to swim with them. Tutu was able to keep an eye on the children from the spot where she was picking the tiny clumps of seaweed.

The children were laughing and jumping in the cold shallows of Kaiaka. Tutu finished plucking the last clump of blood limu from the coral and returned to fetch the children.

As Tutu neared the children, she heard Pua screaming. She dropped her sack and ran toward the children. Keola was pulling Pua into shallower water. As soon as she entered the water, she scooped Pua close to her chest and ran ashore.

On the sand, Tutu searched for the source of Pua's screaming. There was no wound on her granddaughter's entire body. There was no blood anywhere to be found.

Tutu asked Pua, "Where does it hurt?"

Pua opened her closed fist. There were only four fingers. The finger between Pua's middle finger and her pinkie had been bitten off.

CHAPTER 2

Whatever had bitten her had then closed the wound by stapling the loose flesh of her hand with its tooth, sealing the wound. Tutu noticed that the tooth left behind belonged to a shark.

Tutu wrapped Pua's hand in her shirt, carried Pua close to her bosom, and returned quickly to her house.

At home, Tutu put some medicine on Pua's hand. Pua fell over in fatigue. Tutu was not worried because she understood the ways of healing.

After Pua fell asleep, Tutu asked Keola, "What happened?"

Keola put his tiny hand onto his grandmother's ear. "We were playing in the water with our fish. Our fish ate Pua's finger. Scary. I'm afraid of our fish."

"Don't be afraid. Some fish are our family." Tutu comforted Keola. She took the shark's tooth and held it to the light. "We will save this for Pua. I hope that when the time comes, she will remember our god that spoke to her this day," Tutu said. "Come, Keola, let me tell you about Kaleihepule."

A Story from Tutu

The Faith of Kawanana and Kealo

THIS IS THE STORY.

Kawanana was the husband. Kealo was the wife. They lived in the district of Waialua, in the ahupuaa of Anahulu, in the ili of Kaae.

When the waters from Kealo's womb fell, they sent for a woman to help with the birthing. The birthing woman started a fire, but there was no heat. This confused her. She told Kawanana about this extraordinary event.

Kawanana could read omens and he was able to understand the sign. He searched the heavens and he searched the land for further signs.

Kawanana then called for his wife. "My dearest wife, the gods have spoken. You, and you alone, must go to the ocean."

Kawanana and Kealo were not upset. They were not worried. They were not afraid. This is the gift to the religious. Everything is simply placed in the hands of their god.

Kealo made her way down to the sea with some offerings. Her entire body ached. She often became tired during the trip. But she simply followed the directions of her husband and carried the thought of his benevolence.

She arrived at the beach, and sat on the sand. Immediately, the head of the child started to push through.

Kealo dug a hole in the sand because she did not want any sand on the head of her child. She placed her moelua bark cloth inside of the hole. And she waited for her child to come.

CHAPTER 3

Kealo massaged her stomach. The child was not moving. Kealo said to herself, "Perhaps this child will be gentle."

The entire head of the child emerged. With a great push, the entire body followed. The child was not breathing. It was dead.

Kealo had delivered a stillborn child. Great were her tears of sadness. She carried her dead child in her trembling hands.

Kealo's tears fell onto the head of her child. Wherever these tears fell, dark marks were left upon the head of the dead child.

Kealo sat with her child in the water for three days. The child did not stir in the moelua bark cloth.

Kealo was bent over in grief and she chanted:

My dearest child,
My dearest child of the tentacle-like rain
which falls upon the streaked panadanus leaves.
Streaked are my cheeks by my tears,
tears upon the plain of Paalaa,
a plain which is ravaged by the tapa-tearing wind

My dearest child,
child of the river mouth of Anahulu.
Tranquil Anahulu adorned with the kupukupu,
its fragrance visits the nose on the wind,
a wind which blows open the feathers of the apapane,
this honeycreeper chirping a dirge.

My dearest child,
you are esteemed in my affections.
Affections and love of a mother,
a mother bent over in grief and crying.
Crying at never being able to see you again!
Grief! My dearest child!

They went further into the water. And the mother released her child into the ocean wrapped in the moelua tapa cloth.

The head slowly sank into the water, and Kealo slowly uttered a prayer before the gods. Her powerful gods had granted Kealo's prayer.

The favorable Kehau breeze blew. The skin-like surface of the water started to darken, and the waves started to turn.

Kealo looked toward the outer banks of the reef. The child had taken the body of a shark. It was the wondrous power of the gods.

The shark-body moved and the shark's head broke through the water. The shark started to swim hesitantly. Then, it swam in a circle around the legs of its mother. Kealo's body released the placenta. It was the smell that attracted the shark, and it ate the placenta.

Kealo was extremely fatigued but her desire to cleanse herself in the salty water was greater so she scrubbed herself using the sand.

ON THE BANKS OF THE RIVER MOUTH of Anahulu, Kawanana stood. He had brought with him a pig ready for sacrifice, awa, and his moelua tapa cloth to the shark-guardians on the same day that Kealo had gone to the beach.

For three days, he had prayed with the shark-guardians at the coral shrine. Now, his prayers were finished.

Kawanana went into the water with awa and offered it to his new child. He poured the brown liquid into the water and watched as the young shark passed through it again and again until the water was clear again. Then, he gathered his wife in his arms and carried her the entire way back to their house in the uplands.

Portal of the Sun

ON THE DAY I DIED, my mother was so distraught that she thrust her face against a boulder and cracked three teeth. The mix of blood and saliva stained the huge boulder and from then on, that place became known as Bloodstone.

My father gathered me in his arms and brought me to his face. He put his nose against mine and exhaled deeply. He wanted me to share his breath, but I was already gone. He breathed into me again and again, but there was no hope. His tears fell on my face and collected in the corners of my eyes.

My grandmother approached. "He is gone. Give him to me." We disappeared into her garden.

Even though I was dead, I believe I could still smell the clusters of ylang-ylang growing from the trees along the stone boundaries.

She sat under the tall breadfruit tree and began to sing while she wiped the birth fluids off me. White and red placenta fluid covered me.

For a moment, she felt sorrow for the loss of her youth and the loss of her ability to produce and feed life. I could feel the coldness within her, this smaller Darkness within all women. She had felt the deep pangs of motherhood that caused her, for a little while, to forget her song. With her left hand, she picked up some ylang-ylang blossoms, crumpled them in her hand, and inhaled deeply. The sweet, strong smell of the flowers gave her focus and she continued with her song.

I only remember that the garden was a place of strength. I could feel the ribbons of mana coming from all the different trees and shrubs.

The leaves of the huge breadfruit tree in the middle of the garden cast shadows on my face. The long river of mana streamed from the huge trunk into the end of each branch. A light bloomed from the thousands of eyelets from the netlike pattern of the tough skin. Lights of green and red hues poured from the slender and magnificent ti leaves lining the garden. Some of the light shot straight up into the sky and was collected by the thick, dark clouds and released back into the garden. This pathway of mana, this rainbow, immersed the entire area in pink light.

There were no birds chirping. There were no dogs barking. There was only the complete stillness.

The most energy came from the collection of stones partially hidden by the variety of plants at the base of the mango tree. The largest rock pulled all of these energies together and pulsed with a yellow light. It surged with energy, light, and mana. I could feel the energy of the stone pushing into me. The strands of colors filled my eyes, my ears, my navel, and my mouth. The stone was reconnecting me to life by attaching itself to my three umbilical points: the top of my head, my belly, and my genitals. The mana flowed and surged. It pulsed and ebbed. It breathed.

I do not know how long we were in her beautiful garden. The sun had risen to its highest point when the portal of the sun opened. For one very brief moment, I saw the beginning and the end. I saw the infinite strength of ceremony and prayer to open the doors to the spirit world.

I carry the memory of it with me forever. I carry the memory of my grandmother and the words that she uttered to me on that day: "A life for a life I have bargained today. I have bargained yours for another. I love you more than anything and because of this, have given you this curse that will hang over you until it comes true: You will cause the death of your wife and child. I am regretful, but it is a small price for keeping you here."

A cold breeze blew off the ocean and lifted my swaddling blanket. The wind was a fist that rested on my chest. I remember opening my mouth and crying. It was the most favorable moon for planting and the night when children with big eyes were born. It was Hotu.

Beloved Is the Shark, Kaleihepule

KEALO ATE FISH, TARO LEAVES, and dog for a week before she was able to speak. It took her one more month to gain enough strength to walk.

Each morning, Kealo would try to push herself off her sleeping mat, and each time she would cry. She desperately wanted to get to the beach to see her child. Her breasts were filled painfully with milk and reminded her that she had a child that needed her, wanted her, and loved her.

Kawanana went to find the woman who helped with birthing to get medicine to stop the flow of milk, but when he returned to his hut with the bitter medicine, Kealo refused to drink it and pleaded with her husband, "If I drink this, what will our child have to eat? No, you must carry me to the sea."

Kawanana could not refuse his wife. She was his companion of the cold nights and the hot days and there was very little he could deny her. But deep within him was his love for this child. He had prayed three long days and he did not want to insult the gods by letting anything happen to the gift they had given him and his wife.

Kawanana lay next to his wife with his back against her chest and slowly rolled her onto him. He put one leg, then the other, under him and raised himself while gripping the main support pole of their house. He put a rectangle of thin bark cloth over his wife's head to protect her from the sun and started for the beach.

Kawanana carried Kealo to the sea every day for a month. Because the journey took an entire day, there was no time left for tending to his taro patch or garden or fishing in the stream for shrimp. Kawanana and Kealo relied on the help of their families to do their chores and their families did it without complaining.

As soon as Kealo was able, she thought first of making her way to the ocean to see her daughter, Kaleihepule. She got up before the sun had risen and started the fire. She pulled strips of salted fish from the rafters of her thatched house and put them into a small gourd. She softly roused her husband with a tender kick to the pillow that his head was resting on. "Kawanana, I am going to see our child."

"Let me carry you." He stood suddenly.

"No, I'll go alone." She stepped quickly out of the doorway before her husband could protest.

Kealo jumped into the water and, almost immediately, a shape like the moa dart used during makahiki games came swimming toward her. Kealo grasped the dorsal fin and let her daughter take her past the reef flats. "There's only love in my heart for you," Kealo yelled as the saltwater spray flew up from the ocean and trickled down her face.

KEALO WALKED ONTO SHORE. She grabbed some of the dried fish from the gourd container and ate while Kaleihepule jumped out of the water and twisted her body only to fall in again with a splash.

After Kealo had eaten, she called out to Kaleihepule:

Where is my child of Anahulu?
Anahulu of the red hau,
the red cordage that binds the corners,
corners of the house of Pele, Mauliola.

My infant of the reef,
the reef of Puaena,
Puaena of the slanted sea spray,
sea spray that dampens the cheeks.
Where is my sacred child of Anahulu?
It is a request,
to the child of the moelua tapa cloth.
Agree to my request,
I am hungry for flagtail tang.

CHAPTER 5

Kaleihepule swam out to the dark pockets of the coral reef to the various hiding places of the small fish. She chased fish into the skirt of Kealo who picked up the fish and threw them onto the sand.

Kealo walked up to the first fish she had thrown up onto the sand and threw it to Kaleihepule, who swam to the edge of the water. "My love, you are grown enough now, and I cannot come to see you every day. I will come and call for you and will do so until I can convince my husband to move away from his family and closer to the ocean. I will come soon."

She bent over and kissed the shark on its dark spots, picked up the fish and headed toward her home in the uplands.

When Kealo got home, she gave the fish to her husband. "Give this fish to your family with our gratitude for taking care of us while I was sick. Tell them it comes from our family who live near the ocean."

Kaloko

HANALEI KNEW THAT TODAY WAS THE LAST DAY of his life. He had known for some time that he was going to die. It was when one of his gods, Uluhala, a bat that he fed daily with offerings and prayer, appeared in his dream.

In the dream, Uluhala flew and landed on a canoe. The canoe floated in the shallows, filled with provisions for a long journey. When Hanalei approached the canoe, he could see the mounds of clothing among the coconuts, breadfruit, and taro. Hanalei could tell that this was an old koa canoe. It was carved from a single tree and there were no trees that big anymore.

Hanalei lifted his head and took in the coastal landscape of this area. The stunted mountains slid into the ocean in one long, painted stroke. He recognized this beach. He had been here before with his parents and grandmother when he was younger. It was his first introduction to another of the family gods, Kaleihepule.

In the dream, Kaleihepule was there as well. She swam alongside the floating canoe and flicked the surface of the water with her tail. "I will make myself ready," Hanalei told his two gods.

When he opened his eyes from sleep, he thought of the three things that he had to do.

He rose from his bed. He walked quietly into the bathroom and turned on the small light above the bathroom mirror. From the hanger that was nailed onto the back of the bathroom door, he pulled down the clothes that he had arranged the night before. He put on his favorite gingham shorts and his favorite Primo T-shirt. He brushed his teeth and combed his hair with Brilliantine Hair Pomade. Kawika and Hau-nani, his son and daughter-in-law, were still asleep. He took the three wooden steps that led to the backyard, chanted a prayer, and pulled one of the awa plants. He spent the next hour preparing the awa and put the liquid into a thermos. He woke up Kawika. "Son, let's go to Kaloko." Then he went into his grandson's room, and carried the sleeping boy to his white Valiant and started the long trek to Kaloko, on the other side of the island from where they lived.

Witnessing the sunrise over Molokai with his son and grandson was the first of the many things he wanted to do today.

As Kanehoalani began to rise over the eastern part of the ocean, it illuminated the edge of Molokai Island with a filament of golden light. The sky had already turned a deep shade of pink and it changed slowly into a soft yellow light.

HANALEI THOUGHT ABOUT THE TEACHINGS of his grandfather about the rising of the sun. He looked at the peaks behind him to gauge how much time he had before he had to wake his grandson. Hanalei knew that the sun hit the earth at an angle so the peaks of the mountains would illuminate first. He looked at the beach's edge to see if sea birds were venturing out into the sea to catch fish. The dark-rumped petrels were gliding above the fertile channel between Molokai and Oahu. It was a sign that the weather would be sunny and calm. "Yes, this is a good day to have the black tapa cloth pulled over me," Hanalei told himself.

Hanalei woke his grandson in the backseat of his white Valiant. He picked up the thermos and they walked over the rocky shore to the ocean. The sun broke through the cloudless horizon. The sun disc threw shades of reds, yellows, oranges, and pinks onto the ocean and the hills behind Hanalei. Hanalei chanted to the sun:

A flame illuminates Hahaiole.
A light will touch the sands of Kaohikaipu, to fall on Manana.
It will travel toward the mountains and disperse in Luluku,
spreading across the skirt of the Koolau mountains.

I am here now, but never to return.
I travel to the long dark path of Kanaloa
It is!

As Hanalei chanted these words that were given to him by his father, the sun rose completely above the horizon. The intense light made Hanalei's grandson shield his eyes with the sleeve of his jacket. Hanalei was elated by the colors of the sunrise this morning. It was a great beginning for his last day.

KAWIKA KNEW THIS BEACH. He had visited here and chanted with his father a thousand times. Kawika often came here by himself. But when he heard the last line of his father's chant, he bowed his head to hide his tears. "Papa, when?"

"Help me say goodbye to our gods." Hanalei looked toward the sun.

Kawika rose and walked toward his father. The two men chanted in unison and recited the names of all their gods. Then they recited the names of their entire family. Kawika put his left hand on the shoulder of his father, and watched as the morning portal of the sun closed. There were two more portals left, midday and sunset.

Hanalei got out of the water and walked straight to the car. He thought about the many times that he had come to this beach, the many times he had seen the sun rise, and the many people that he had met on this stretch of sand and ocean. However, in all those trips, in all those chance meetings, he never met anyone he wanted to be. He never regretted that he was a Hawaiian, and he knew that made all the difference in the world.

Even though Hanalei knew he was going to die today, he wanted it to be just like any other day. He ate a simple meal of soda crackers with peanut butter, a banana from his garden, and a cup of hot cocoa. He cleaned out his small room in the home that he shared with his son, his daughter-in-law, and his grandson. It was important to him that his death not be a burden to his family.

He packed all his clothes and put them into large, brown trash bags except for the aloha shirt his beloved wife, Honey, had bought him for Christmas from Liberty House before she died. He also set

aside his favorite pair of crisp white slacks. "They can bury me in this."
He smiled.

The only thing he could not bear to pack were the photos of his
wife. He had been married to Honey for forty-three years before she
died of cancer. She was his companion in the cold, and the mother of
his children. She helped him collect salt from the rocky coast of Kaiaka, and packed lunches of pork and beans and mango when they went
to the beach.

Even though she came frequently to him in his dreams to talk and
laugh, he looked forward to holding her large body in his arms again.
"We're going to live it up tonight, Honey. I hope you're making me a
pot of your beef stew."

Hanalei tied the bags with the rest of his clothing and placed the
sacks in the tin-roofed shed in the back. He exhaled slowly as he surveyed the contents of the shed: fishing nets that he had used to catch
young trevally and goatfish, iron thongs that he used to pull sea urchins out of their holes, and an old, large metal pail surrounded by
inflated inner tubes that floated on the surface of the ocean and held
his catch.

Hanalei looked at the sky and he knew the second portal would
be opening soon. The portal that opened at midday was the most important portal. It opened the doorway between the worlds of people and
the world of the spirits, and if the correct protocols were performed, the
gods showed their favor by conversing with the haka.

It was in a ceremony in Pohakea at midday, over fifty years ago,
that he received the guardianship of all the aumakua. The intense heat
of the sun had burned his body that day. It sat on his head like a crown.
The heat was so bitter that it was hard to focus on the ceremony. But he
did. When it was his turn to recite the names of the aumakua, to call
them to him, he struggled. He did not want to offend any of these gods
by mispronouncing any of their names or, worse, by forgetting one of
them. He rallied in spite of the heat. He called out their names: Uluhala,
his bat aumakua; and Kaleihepule, his shark aumakua. The midday portal opened and he was bombarded with visions. The heat of the sun had
transported him through the portal. Bats started to fly around his head.
Hanalei stood and received the gift from the other side of the portal.

Hanalei had already given the care of the aumakua to his son. He knew they would be safe. Hanalei looked up. The sun was directly overhead. He looked across at all the tools that had made up his life, made his eyes wander once more inside this humble shed, and closed this door for the last time.

Hanalei walked up the three steps to the back door of his house. Even before he opened the screen door, he smelled warm mango bread. "Papa, I made some lunch. Let's go riding today." Haunani put the last stone into the cavity of the chicken before tying it up with leaves of the ti plant.

"Good. I'll take some awa for us." Hanalei searched under the wooden kitchen cupboards for an empty plastic gallon container.

By the time they got to the beach, the tiny, hot rocks had cooked the large chicken. The smell of the chicken cooking made the entire family salivate during the entire ride.

The sea spray from the waves was a smoky film over the rocky flats. Haunani took the large green army blanket from the car and spread it out over the sand. Kawika took out his portable radio. It was stuck on the same radio station, KCCN, and only played Hawaiian music. The plastic latch that holds the batteries had broken off a long time ago but Kawika used a huge rubber band to hold them in.

Hanalei got out of the car, took out the fishing poles, and walked toward the rocks. "Eh boy, bring the can of bait. Let's set these up before we eat."

Grandfather and grandson tied the morsels of bloody fish to the hooks and cast them into the crests of waves that were breaking on the reef. The grandson copied the way his grandfather arched his pole over his shoulder before snapping the pole and watching the hook plop into the water. When the poles were placed and held firmly in the steel pipes that had been cemented into the rocks, they headed back to shore.

Hanalei took his grandson's hand and led him onto the sandy section of the beach. He bent over, and motioned the young boy to get onto his back. They entered the water together until Hanalei was waist-deep. He began a chant that had been taught to him by his father and was probably as old as the ocean itself:

A calm sea, a moving sea is the channel of Kaiaka.
There, perhaps a floating island from Polihale, made sacred by
    Aiaiakuulakai.
Where are you my child of Anahulu?
Anahulu of the red hau, of the red hau cordage
the cordage that binds the corners
the corners of the house of Pele, Mauliola.
My infant of the reef
the reef of Puaena,
Puaena of the slanted sea spray
sea spray that dampens the cheeks.
Where is my sacred child of Anahulu?
A kahu calls out,
to the child of the moelua tapa cloth,
to the child of the makaula tapa cloth.
Agree to my prayer! A kahu calls out to you,
I hunger for turtle.

Hanalei and his grandson watched as a black shark appeared in one of the waves. They could clearly see its fin above the surface. It rode so close to the top of the water that they could see one of its eyes. The grandson became excited and afraid at the same time and tried to climb higher onto his grandfather's back so that neither of his legs were in the water. Hanalei comforted him. "It's okay—that's our family, Kaleihepule."

The shark dove into the water and was not seen again for three minutes. But when it did emerge from the dark blue water, it was chasing a turtle. It dodged from left to right, and left again to cut off the turtle from escaping, and made the huge female lodge itself in the shallows by nipping its rear left flipper. The shark had also become stranded on the exposed reef, but it used its tail to dislodge and propel itself back into the ocean. Grandfather and grandson looked into its large black eyes before it jumped back into the water. Salt water dripped from the large eyes and, for a few seconds, it appeared to be crying.

"Kawika, grab the turtle!" Hanalei pointed to the female that tried to turn around and crawl back into the deep water. Kawika sprang toward the turtle and flipped her on her back. Hanalei put his grandson on the beach and helped his son carry the large turtle to the shore. He took out his knife and started to carve the turtle in sections so it could fit into the cooler. He first removed the head, then the carapace.

Hanalei searched for the tender organs. He pulled the liver and the heart from the green fat that lined the interior of the body cavity, walked over to the ocean, and threw the choice morsels in front of the shark. The shark gulped the offerings. Then Hanalei took the awa and poured it into the water. Kaleihepule swam up to the cloudy water and passed through it repeatedly. Hanalei took off his shirt and jumped into the water. He stood in the shallow water and used some shells to scrape the barnacles off her back and head. When he was done, he placed his hand on Kaleihepule's fin and they glided together through the water. He had been her guardian and priest for fifty-two years; she had been with him during lean times and during good times. She had even saved his life. Now, on this day, they were saying goodbye to each other for the very last time.

Hanalei kneeled in the water. He pulled Kaleihepule up to him, and gave her a deep honi. "My deepest love," he uttered. He kissed her head and walked up to the beach. He could not bear to look at her for the last time, but he knew that Kaleihepule was watching him.

Kawika watched his father swim in the water with Kaleihepule. All his life, Kawika had been comforted by the idea that his father loved him more than anyone else in the world. This unconditional love was a strong foundation that allowed him to try new things, to love others, and to weather challenges. Whenever he walked into his father's presence, he saw the way his father's eyes lit up. Even though Hanalei loved others, Kawika knew that he loved him more than anyone or anything else in this world. Kawika did not want to think about his father's death. If he did, if he allowed even the tiniest thought to enter his mind, he would fling himself onto the sharp rocks that lined the beach.

Instead, Kawika busied himself with preparing the turtle. He cut the tender inside of the turtle into strips, and threw them into a container of salt water. Haunani built a fire in a pit of sand using twigs, sticks, and coconut fiber. She placed large white coral directly in the fire and watched the porous rocks turn a soft pink from the heat. As soon as the rocks were hot enough, she placed the turtle strips on the coral and cooked them until the fat around the edges bubbled from the heat of the fire.

Kawika used the sand to scrub the inside of the turtle shell. When it was clean, he put the turtle shell in the trunk of his car. He would shellac it, polish it, and hang it in his garage with the other turtle shells.

Haunani pulled open the ti-leaf bundle, and the chicken fell apart into its own juices. She set the bundle on the foldout table with the bowl of poi, the strips of turtle, the wedges of steamed breadfruit from home, and the two fish they had caught. She made a small plate for her son. "Don't only eat turtle. Eat some breadfruit too." The family smiled at each other and ate noisily. Hanalei relished every morsel.

Even though it was starting to get chilly, Hanalei insisted on staying at the beach until sunset. He wanted to see the sun set over Kaena one final time. He knew that he needed to be ready when the last portal opened.

The family watched in silence as the sun started to set. Soon, the sun had descended crookedly into the pocket of the water. As the sun was halfway in the water, Hanalei placed his grandson on his lap and whispered into his ear, "Papa loves you very much."

"I love you too, Papa," was the very last thing that Hanalei heard in this world. His soul lifted from his body and flew toward Kaena, to Keaokuukuu, where it would jump off the rocky point into the sun portal. He was hoping to see his family so they could help him enter the land of the spirits.

Hanalei reached the top of Keaokuukuu. Standing at the edge of the cliff were generations of family: his sister, parents, grandparents, great-grandparents, and ancestors. He had never met some of them but now, all of them welcomed him and made sure that he did not fall into the abyss, the darkness of eternal wandering. They led him into the portal of the sun before it closed.

He entered the portal.

There were so many rewards in life. It was very hard to leave. Even as he lay dying, he thought of resisting Death. He thought of grasping and holding onto something that would tie him to the world he had known for over sixty years. As the final moment approached, as he was about to leave his physical body behind, he cuddled his grandson one more time.

Death was Hanalei's greatest happiness because he knew that it was his time. But it was the hardest thing he had ever had to do. Finally, in those last moments of clarity as Death started to take his body, he separated. He separated from his body. He separated from his life. He separated from this love.

Hanalei plunged himself completely into the portal and everything for his soul was light and dark at the same time.

The Dark

PUA STOOD AT THE SQUARE BATHROOM MIRROR with her left hand held up to her face. She did this every morning of every day of every week of every month of every year for the last ten years since she had been bitten.

Mornings were the only time she looked into the mirror. And, on this morning—like the hundreds that came before it—there was the real danger that she could have gotten caught up in her imperfect reflection and refused to turn away from the square mirror in her grandmother's bathroom, in her grandmother's modest home, encircled by her grandmother's beautiful gardens. On that day, if she so chose, Pua could have escaped into herself forever like so many others who bear the pain of humiliation and deformity.

But as she retreated, a long, invisible tendril wrapped itself around her and did not permit Pua to detach from herself. This umbilical cord connected Pua with her ancestors. She was not ready. There was so much to learn. Still, so much more to learn.

KEOLA STOOD ON THE BRANCH OF THE MANGO TREE in the middle of the yard and looked east at the huge gray slates of smoke rising from the flash of yellow flames eating the crops of sugarcane. The yearly burn was a treat for the entire community as families sat on the roofs of their houses and watched the black smoke rise into the sky. It was his favorite time of the year.

Keola slid down the mango tree and ran into the house. "Pua, let's go watch the fire from the bridge."

Pua's spirit shifted back into her, then she yelled, "I cannot. I have to get goat's milk for Tutu. You cannot go either—you have to drive me."

Keola pulled the keys for the Mazda and ran outside. He checked to make sure that all the ropes were tied securely around the tires of the car to keep the inside tubes from shifting. Brown rust had almost consumed the car. The fabric that lined the ceiling of the car was tied with string to prevent it from falling on their heads.

Pua got into the car and watched as Keola opened the door, grabbed the door frame, pushed, and jumped in. As the car rolled down the hill, he jump-started the engine. Pua told him, "We need to go to Kahuku to buy two goats."

Keola winced. He really wanted to go to the bridge to watch the sugarcane burn. When he was younger, Tutu would give Keola ten cents to go to the corner gas station to buy soda for him and Pua. Tutu made popcorn and the three of them walked to the bridge and watched the huge fire while drinking Pepsi and eating Jiffy popcorn. He just loved the immensity of the thick, gray smoke as it spread over his tiny community. But most of all, he loved these shared moments with the two people that he loved most in the world, his grandmother and his cousin, Pua.

When they arrived in Kahuku at the goat farmer's house, Keola let the car run while Pua gave the Chinese man two dollars and took the two milking goats that he had tethered to the ironwood tree.

"Let's go." Pua put the two goats into the back of the Mazda.

She slid into the front passenger's seat from the driver's side. Keola followed and turned the Mazda back onto the dusty road.

KEOLA PULLED THE LARGER DOELING TOWARD him by grabbing onto her horns. "Damned goats," he muttered when he saw the green goat marbles all over the backseat. He lifted her onto the ground, pulled her over to the clothesline pole, and tied her up with a rusty dog chain that was hanging from the mango tree.

Keola walked back to the car to get the other goat when he saw the smaller doeling following Pua to the backyard. "She likes your smell," he laughed. "Looks like you got a friend."

CHAPTER 7

Pua was insulted and she picked up a dry stick to throw at Keola but stopped midswing. Her eyes became large as the reality of what she was seeing became increasingly plausible. Keola saw the fear in Pua's eyes and he became afraid as well.

"What is it? What is it, cousin?" He turned slowly and looked over the fence of ti leaves that divided the west side of Tutu's yard from the home of the Akina family.

He ducked as the first bat screeched over his head. The second bat hit him on the back of his neck with its left wing before losing its balance and tumbling to the ground. Keola's dog, Kolohe, bit into it and dragged it under the house. Keola ran and covered Pua with his body.

The bats continued to come. The entire sky was peppered with hundreds of flying black specks that loomed right above Tutu's home.

The mass shifted together and flew, clockwise, around Tutu's house three times before making one final, deafening shriek. Pua closed her eyes and covered her left ear with her hand while burying her right ear in Keola's chest. She remained this way until there was no noise.

Pua and Keola stood quietly. They knew that an event such as this was a sign of something big.

They took a step apart from each other and the first thought they each had was to run and call their grandmother. But as they turned to do so, they saw Tutu on the porch. She took one step forward and her legs buckled under her. Her right hand reached for something that was not there. She reached out, repeatedly, trying to grasp something that only she could see.

In the next instant, a sound of grief came out of her tiny but strong body. It was a wail of pain and sorrow.

Keola and Pua ran to their grandmother. They put their hands under her arms and tried to lift her, but she fought back. She pushed them away with such force that Pua fell off the porch and into the clump of cherry tomatoes. Keola lost his balance and fell backward into the pile of slippers and Japanese cotton foot coverings on the right side of the door.

The Breath of Crabs

IT HAD BEEN OVER THREE HOURS since the bats had flown over her home. The large, dark mass had scared the grandchildren. Tutu was in shock. There was only one reason why Uluhala would fly over her house and it was not good. Her life energy altered and she could still feel the rupture within her. A life of another had been lost today. She had felt it slowly flickering until it extinguished completely.

At first, Tutu thought it was her heart, an annoying reminder that she was old. Then she had thought that it was her stomach telling her that she was hungry. But as the energy started to dim, she stepped outside her house to look for signs of the Shifting. What she saw had horrified her and had ripped the breath out of her small body.

Tutu had screamed so loud and with such passion and hurt that the dogs stopped barking. Keola and Pua had never heard such a scream from Tutu. They thought she was terrified by the colony of bats that had circled their house. She fell on the porch and had refused help for over an hour.

When she stopped crying, she went into the house, took a shower, and put on her most favorite dress. She had brushed her hair, braided the silver length, and coiled the braid at the back of her head. She went into the garden, pulled some red and yellow plumeria flowers from her tree, and bobby-pinned them into her bun. She appeared rested and calm, but she refused food.

Tutu sat in her favorite chair. The leather from the recliner was tattered and ripped so she had quilted a cover made from tiny squares of

Japanese cloth remnants from Woolworth's. Her mind drifted to her youth and her parents. When she thought of them, she could no longer control herself and cried. She stared out the large bay window at the Mohalu moon and waited for her Kawika to call.

"Tutu, have some mamaki tea." Keola placed the large mug on the koa table next to the recliner. Keola looked at his grandmother and wanted to reach out and protect her. She was not a fragile woman by any means but she appeared to be without hope. He had no idea what the bats were about, although he felt that their arrival portended something. He had lived with his Tutu his entire life. He knew to wait until she was ready to explain. Everything would make sense when it needed to make sense. This was how his universe worked.

Tutu knew that her twin, Hanalei, had died. She felt him leave. Now, she was waiting for her nephew to call her to tell her that her twin was dead.

She knew that her nephew was preparing his house for her visit. She knew that the body needed to be cleaned and prepared. She knew they needed time and so she waited for news that she already knew. She asked Keola and Pua to prepare some food and to pack it in containers.

When the telephone rang at seven, Tutu answered it on the first ring. "Aloha."

"Tutu, Papa passed this evening. He left just as the sun sank near Kaena. You are the first family we called," said the voice on the phone.

"I will come right over, Kawika," Tutu responded. It took all her strength to place the phone back in the cradle. She headed into the kitchen to gather the food to take over to Kawika's house.

WHEN TUTU, PUA, AND KEOLA got to Kawika's home, the family came outside to greet them. The matriarch of the family had arrived and they were anxious for her visit. Tutu opened the car door, pulled her sweater close to her, and stepped out. As she faced her brother's family she began to chant. The breeze that was coming off the ocean carried her lament:

Across the ili of Kamaile
travels the Maeaea wind and the Keawe rain.
The tentacle rain of Haleiwa

that snatches the cold in Waialua.
It is the twin waters of Waialua
that diverge into the salty sea,
the salty sea of Kaiaka
a favorite grounds for octopus.
We will sew a lei of shells
from the sands of Pupukea.
A place where we climbed
to the heights to Puu Mahuka.
We are bent over in grief
a grief that brings tears.
Tears that fall down our cheeks, leaving streaks
Streaks like the leaf-patterns on the panadanus that grows near
    the sea.
He is gone. Aue.

Tutu walked slowly to her brother's children. The weight of Tutu's words saddened Kawika and Haunani. They began to cry. Kawika jumped off the family lanai and ran into Tutu's arms. "Aunty. We grieve."

"Yes, my love. We cry together." Tutu wiped his tears from his face as Keola and Pua hugged Haunani. The family members hugged and kissed each other. They bemoaned not getting together more often. And they promised each other to visit more often. Time stood still in their grief until Tutu decided that she needed to see her twin. "Kawika, take me to see my brother."

Kawika led Tutu into the living room where Hanalei lay. Kawika had meticulously dressed his father. Hanalei was wearing his favorite white pants and aloha shirt from Liberty House. The long-sleeved aloha shirt was a burgundy-and-white floral print. His hands were along his sides and a lace throw covered him. Kawika had generously applied pomade to Hanalei's hair and combed every strand into place. Tutu could see that even Hanalei's fingernails and toenails were clipped. She smiled as she thought of Kawika's consideration for her brother and put her head on Hanalei's chest.

As soon as Tutu's head touched Hanalei's chest, flashes of their life together made her eyes tear. She remembered their time together in her mother's womb and how they loved when their mother drank sweet coconut milk. She remembered their childhood together in Paalaa. Even though they had twelve other siblings, Tutu and Hanalei had been adopted at birth by their maternal grandparents. The grandparents asked for the child in their mother's womb as soon as she began to crave whale fat. They were not surprised when she gave birth to twins. As soon as they were five years old, Tutu's grandmother and grandfather trained them to be doctors and to take care of their gods.

Tutu laughed to herself when she remembered when her grandmother dried octopus in the sun. They would tear off the legs because they were so delicious. "I hope you are eating all the dried octopus that you can eat, brother." She rubbed his stomach.

The entire family pretended that they were chatting among themselves. They were watching Tutu and their hearts were breaking. The sight of one twin saying goodbye to the other was more than they could handle. Their entire beings were consumed with sadness because they started to think of the person they loved the most, and how they would handle it if that person died.

Tutu kissed her brother. She touched his cheek and stood up. "Kawika, holy moly, you put too much pomade in my brother's hair. Let's take some of it off before your Aunty Leilani says something."

The entire family burst into laughter. A deep laughter shook the foundations of the small gray house next to the ocean. In an instant, as much as they grieved about the passing of Hanalei, they started to celebrate life. There was happiness and stories. There were old stories that had been heard many times before and new stories that were heard for the first time.

"Kawika, it is time to call the rest of the family." Tutu touched his arm tenderly. Kawika called his sister and cousins and aunty and granduncles. For two days, the family streamed in and out of the small family home.

Kawika had forgotten how many cousins he had. There were so many cousins. He had not seen many of them since he was young. They all came to pay their respects. His house was as full as it could possibly be. There were children everywhere.

Haunani spent the entire day cooking and talking with the women in the kitchen. Some of the cousins went diving and came back with parrotfish, octopus, lobsters, unicorn fish, and sea urchins. There were vats of beef stew, chicken with long rice, and octopus in taro leaves.

Hanalei was in the middle of it all. The elderly women wept while putting their hands on his face. They would take turns fanning the body and stroking his hair. When the women were not looking, two of Kawika's nephews, Hano and Kamuela, went up to Hanalei and pried his eyes open. Aunty Lulu came out of the bathroom and saw what those two boys were up to. She snuck up to them while they focused on Hanalei's eyes. She raised her hand and slapped both of them across the back of the neck. "Rotten kids, get outside!" They screamed in fright and ran to their mothers.

Their mothers had no pity for such insolent boys. They were sent outside and told to stay there.

Keola and Pua took care of the young children, washed dishes, and did whatever else they were told to do. In times like these, the younger generation was expected to find the work that needed to be done and to do it.

TUTU ROSE EARLY ON THE MORNING of the third day. She went out to the lanai to wait for the sun as it began to rise and was greeted by a cool wind that was coming off the ocean. When she looked into the darkness, she could make out the figure of Kawika sitting on the steps. "Nephew, what are you doing?"

"Just sitting down. Kaleihepule has refused to come since Papa died." Kawika stood and kissed Tutu on the cheek. Tutu held onto Kawika. "Kaleihepule needs to guide his soul to where it needs to go. She will come back when she is ready," Tutu reassured him.

"I miss Dad," Kawika said, and turned toward the ocean.

"I miss him too." Tutu took his arm in hers. As she finished speaking, a strong, salty breeze blew through the lanai.

"When the waves recede, the crabs come out of their holes to breathe. They have only a few seconds to breathe before the next wave comes and forces them back into their holes. This entire stretch of beach has thousands of crabs. All of them have this same rhythm. Wave after wave comes and they only have a little window to take what they need to survive. We have to keep going in spite of the things that happen to us because we are Hawaiian. Wave after wave. Breath after breath. The salty, salty breeze is a sign that the cycle is still going. We can learn a lot from even the littlest things if we pay attention. It is important to look for lessons, even in the breath of crabs."

Answers in the Forest

TUTU KNEW RIGHT AWAY THAT she was dreaming. Whenever there was something that was bothering her, she dream-traveled into the forest. Once she got there, she knew that he would be waiting.

She flew into the forest headfirst, past the cluster of ohia and shards of ferns hanging from the tall pillars of lama. She knew every tree in this forest by name. Her own life and death were carved into the skin of these giants: the acacia, the ebony, the bamboo, and the mountain apple among them.

When the wind pushed the bamboo into each other, the long, deep, moaning sound made her remember how afraid she had been to come here when she was younger. Now, as their deep, penetrating shadows threw odd shapes onto the forest floor and their long branches held up the canopy, she was grateful for these solitary walks. This forest was old and she had started learning its secrets before her first menses.

She was now approaching her seventh decade of living. Her legs were still strong. She could still reason. Her eyes were still clear. Her hearing was better than a sand crab's. There was always the one lesson that had remained with her since she started coming here with her grandfather: each tree was a life. What one took, one had to repay in kind.

She looked ahead and could see a clearing of aalii and remembered the saying:

CHAPTER 9

The aalii that remains upright in the wind.

SHE KNEW THAT HE WOULD BE THERE, just past the short wall of aalii that was now turning into the dark red colors that hula schools like to use. She set her feet down into the wet mud of the forest floor and hurried quickly to the house that was made of pili. She knew it was there, past the tall wall of bamboo. She had visited it a hundred times before. She pulled her nightgown closer to her and followed the narrow path.

The man seated by the fire turned slowly toward her. "Granddaughter, I am for a long time now in the land of souls. Why do you bring me back?"

"I came looking for Hanalei," she replied.

"He will come to you when you need him."

"Keola has learned all that he can from me," Tutu said. "I need help to make him the best doctor that he can be."

The old man turned toward the moon.

"He must go on a journey. You must send him to your cousin that lives in Waianae."

"I don't know if Keola is ready."

"You have no choice. It has been decided." The grandfather poked the embers of the fire with a stick.

They talked until her soul pressed her to return to her body.

The Surf Beckons

KEALO DID NOT TELL KAWANANA she was pregnant. "How typical for him not to notice that I did not go to the menstrual house for the last two months," she mumbled as she tied the ribs of pili together for roof thatching.

Her right hand collected grass blades that were the same length and put them together in her left hand. When the bunch was just large enough that she could touch her third finger together with her thumb, she tied braided sennit around the base and tossed it into the pile. The dried grass was making her nose itch and she was sure not to make too much of a commotion because she did not want the dried dust to get into her already-itching eyes.

This was such wearisome work. Kealo did not want to tie pili bundles underneath the candlenut all day. Kealo wanted to go to the beach to let the cool water cover her body. She wanted to wade in the water and pick seaweed to eat. She wanted to swim with her child. She wanted to surf!

Kawanana had told her that they needed to repair the roofs before the next rains came. She knew it too, but how delicious it was to take some time off to play.

Realizing that she needed to finish the bundles before Kawanana came home with more pili, she resigned herself to her work. To pass the time, she started to sing a song about surfing locations and an excellent surfer:

CHAPTER 10

A large swell for
Maunalua
Paiko
Kawaikui
Wailupe
Waiale
Kahala
Kaikoo
Kuilei
Waikiki
Kalehuawehe
Aiwohi
Maihiwa
Kapuni
Kuhio
Kahaloa
Kalia
Mamala
Kakaako
Kewalo
Honolulu
Keehi
Ewa
Oneula
Kalaeloa
Kahe
Puu o Huhu
Ulehawa
Maipalaoa
Maili
Lualualei
Kaneilio
Lohilohi
Makaha
Kepuhi
Keeau

Pukano
Popaia
Kaena
Mokuleia
Kaiaka
Alii
Paalaa
Puaena
Papailoa
Laniakea
Puu Nenua
Waimea
Haeula
Pupukea
Kalalau
Waena
Ehukai
Kaunala
Waiale
Kawela
Kuilima
Honohonu
Kahuku
Laie
Hauula
Kanenalu
Heleloe
Kailua
Makapuu
Waimanalo
Wawamalu
Kealahou
Kawaihoa
and Kokokai
That's it!

A swell near the gushing waters of Waikiki beckons the expert.

Perhaps she should grasp her long board of koa wood with two hands and plunge into the waters of Kuhio?

That's it!

PERHAPS SHE SHOULD POINT THE BOARD ma uka toward the grove of large coconut to sip the sweet waters.

No! She should point the board toward the water, towards the surf of Kalehuawehe and if they ask, "Are you skilled at surfing?"

She will ride the board until it is broken.

That's it!

KEALO LAUGHED UNCONTROLLABLY.

"Wife, why are you laughing? Is it that much fun to bundle pili?"

Kealo got up and ran to kiss her husband. "I am so tired of this work. Can we go to the ocean and surf?"

Kawanana looked at Kealo with concern and put the huge bunch of pili down on the pandanus mat next to Kealo. "How can you think of surfing when you are pregnant?"

Kealo took him in her arms. "Husband, that is the reason I am in this state. I cannot concentrate. Come, let's play with the surfboard called Olo."

Kawanana laughed at his wife. "Wife, let me go to the river to wash off this dirt."

"Hurry!"

The cool water will be great, Kawanana said to himself as he walked the short path to the river flowing from the uplands. He could hear the rushing water and decided to run the rest of the way.

As Kawanana approached the river, he saw two foreigners standing on the path looking toward the mountains. They were both dressed in stifling, dark clothing. Kawanana tried to walk around them.

Occasionally, foreigners would come into the area but Kawanana did not associate with them. He mistrusted them not because they had ever done anything bad to him, but because their appearance was different, and they spoke differently. He wondered why they did not prefer to stay in their own lands.

When they saw him approach, they extended their hands, but Kawanana did not respond in kind.

One of the men said in Hawaiian, "Greetings. We are looking for Kawanana. Do you know where we can find him?" Kawanana was startled by the fact that they knew his name. What did these two foreigners want with him, he asked himself. However, he decided to continue on his way. The two men were startled and became indignant at this rudeness.

Kawanana reached the river and slid into the cold. Once he rinsed off, he swam up to a cluster of shampoo ginger flowers and squeezed the flowers until the soapy liquid came out. He used this to clean himself. While he was washing his hair, he thought of the two men he had seen on the path to the river. Kawanana decided that one man was a teacher and the other was his student. He could tell this from the way that they interacted. When he had first seen them, one man was pointing toward the cliffs while the other was writing.

There was a marked difference in their age. It had been the older one who had spoken to Kawanana. It was also his stature. The older man stood straight and was sure of himself. The younger man was slightly hunched over and less assured. But still it did not account for who these men were. What did they want?

Kawanana pulled himself out of the river, dried himself off, and put on a fresh malo. He decided to take the longer path that ran parallel with the river so as not to run into the same men again. They gave him an uneasy feeling, he had finally admitted to himself, and he wanted to talk to others of the village about these two. The swim in the cold river had rejuvenated him. He hurried to see Kealo.

As Kawanana came over the hill to his home, he saw his brother in front of his home with his wife. His brother was talking to the two men. "What is this?" he spat as he approached them.

"Hi, Kawanana." The brothers neared to exchange breaths. "This man has traveled from the big village to meet you." He mouthed the words with some difficulty. "He says his name is David Forbes. He says that he is making a tour of the islands and is interested in learning about burials and wishes to talk to you."

"Tell him to go back to where he is from," Kawanana said harshly. "If I see him around here poking around our burials, I will kill him."

Kawanana looked at his brother. "Our family's bones are not to be exposed to the sun."

Kawanana left abruptly and with purpose. If he did not leave those men, he was likely to get violent. He had heard of men such as these who plundered grave sites, took everything that was within them, and sold it to collectors. He let these men go because he had no proof of any wrongdoing. But he also did not have the patience to talk to them. Let their descendants suffer the repercussions of his actions.

Wrath of the Centipedes

AFTER HANALEI'S FUNERAL, TUTU STAYED IN HER ROOM for a month. The self-imposed confinement was an effort to heal from the deep loss that she felt for her twin.

Because she was a healer, there was no way that she could face the multitudes of people who sought her care. If she was not in good health then she could hurt the very ones that she was trying to heal. Everyone felt her absence.

Pua needed an explanation for the dreams that came to terrorize her night after night. It would always begin and end in the same way: Pua was standing on the Anahulu seashore. The water was still. There was no wind—not even the Hapailau wind was present. She stared off into the distance; she could make out the outline of a two-seat canoe. As the canoe neared the shore, she could see the figure of a young man paddling the canoe. As he neared, Pua's face began to feel warm. She could see his face and she was instantly attracted to him. In the second seat of the canoe, she could make out the figure of an old man who was carrying a basket woven from the leaves of the coconut. When the canoe touched the shore, the old man stayed in the canoe while the young man jumped out of the canoe and onto the sand. The handsome man neared Pua and reached out to touch her face. As his hand came closer, Pua could see that it was made of centipedes. She screamed as the long whip of centipedes stung her face again and again. They stung her eyeballs from their sockets and crawled into them. She felt the tiny legs dig their way into her flesh. They crawled into her nose, ears, and mouth. They crawled into her throat and wriggled into her belly where they stung her over and over again. She doubled over in agony. When she awoke, her face was stinging.

For an entire month, these dreams tortured Pua. She wanted to tell Tutu but she could not put herself before her grandmother. Nor could she tell Keola. Her dream embarrassed her. She had never felt the attraction to a man before. But here she was, now, feeling desire and pain for a person she had never met. She was falling in love with a dream—one that brought her warmth and one that brought her pain. Something told her that as much as she loved Keola, this was not something that she could share with him.

WHILE TUTU TOOK THE TIME to heal her soul, Keola took care of all her medicinal herbs, fruits, and plants. Each day he pruned the weeds that grew in the pockets between the medicinal plants. He watered the organized tangle of Spanish moss and picked any of the mango, guava, banana, and breadfruit that had ripened. If there were too many fruits for their small household of three, he would place some of the fruits on the rock wall that fronted their house. He knew that the children passing by on their way to school would eat them. No food was ever wasted.

"Aloha," Mrs. Helekunihi beckoned Keola with her hand. "Is your Tutu here?"

Keola walked toward her. "Aloha. Sorry, but she is not feeling well today." He offered, "Maybe I can help you with something."

"I have brought your Tutu some fish from my house. I was hoping that she could come over to visit my husband," Mrs. Helekunihi whimpered.

"Is it his legs again?" Keola asked.

"Yes."

"Okay. Let me prepare some things and I will be right over."

Keola ran into the yard to the short bush with bright yellow flowers. He uttered his prayer to his god and asked that his hand pick the best plants to heal the gout of Mr. Helekunihi. After his prayer, with his right hand he picked some leaves, buds, and flowers. He walked into the kitchen and stood in front of the huge double sink. The sink, like the rest of the house, was immaculate. Tutu healed people in this house and she demanded a clean house. Gingerly, he ran the plants under the faucet to clean off the dirt and bugs. He reached under the sink and grabbed the small medicine pounder. This lighter one made of marble had replaced an old one made of stone. It was too heavy for Tutu.

He stripped the leaves from the bark, tore apart the buds and the flowers, and ground them together. When it was a mash, he added a few splashes of water until it was a drink. He reached around the counter and pulled a sieve made from handkerchief material and squeezed the juice from the ground plant. Keola poured the liquid into a thermos. He uttered a prayer of thanks that the medicine had been prepared correctly and lifted it to his lips to test the potency.

The medicine was good. Keola placed the medicine on the counter and went into the living room to look for Pua. She was chewing small pieces of awa root.

"I am going to the Helekunihi home. I will be back in a few hours," Keola told his cousin. He was careful not to make any negative gestures or make any mention of illness because to do so would have added negative energy to Pua's healing process. He knew that she was making some medicine for Tutu. And he knew from her face that she was especially intent on making sure that everything in this medicine was made correctly.

Keola gathered the thermos with the medicine and headed over to the Helekunihi residence. He smiled.

It was hard not to take for granted the peace and love that he shared with Tutu and Pua. At that moment, there were only three of them in the world, and Keola was the luckiest man alive.

AS TUTU LAY ON HER BED, she felt that she was the luckiest woman in this corner of God's Eden. The routine of preparing medicine was instilled in every fiber of her being; and she knew it intimately in the same way that she knew breathing or eating. Without even looking in the living room or in the kitchen, she knew that her granddaughter was preparing awa. She could tell it was awa by the way that it sounded as it was snapped into smaller pieces. She could also tell that her grandson was in the kitchen preparing medicine for Mr. Helekunihi's gout. She had heard Mrs. Helekunihi approach the front as Keola was watering the plants. Her visit was followed by Keola's entering the house, pounding what was surely the leaves and flowers of the bidens, and then the sound he made as he reached for the sieve that was hanging over the counter. She heard the tender, loving exchange that went on between Keola and Pua and she knew that the love they shared would outlast her stay on earth. She knew that the knowledge of plants, medicine, and people would continue long after she was gone and for that she was especially grateful.

Tutu was not grateful for the paths that they would take to get there. She was especially worried for the signs that told her that there would be trials ahead. Her intuition and her gods in the spirit world could not tell her the nature of these trials but she was sure that they were coming soon. And as she lay in bed, she willed the strength back into her body. Bit by bit, she pushed her body to cede to the demands of her will. She was still grieving for her twin. She would miss Hanalei until the day that she died. They shared their own language that even their other brother and sisters could not understand. They alone were given the care of the gods because from a young age they had exhibited traits that the elders knew were special. Just as she had chosen Keola and Pua to carry on and build upon her knowledge. But, for now, she had to be strong. She would meet her brother in the spirit world again. But her grandchildren needed her now in this one.

TUTU AWOKE. THERE WERE TWISTING AND TURNING noises and muffled screams coming from Pua's room. Tutu had waited to diagnose the cause of these dreams. If it had only been once, then perhaps Pua had eaten orange goatfish. If it had been more than once, then perhaps Pua had forgotten to ceremonially cleanse herself after treating a patient. Tutu was sure that her nightmares had continued for at least a week. Today, Tutu decided to find out what it was.

Tutu got up and put her feet on the wooden floor. "Pua, I am ready for you."

"Coming, Tutu." Pua entered the small, immaculate bedroom.

After the prayers had been uttered and she took her morning medicines, Tutu gathered her most precious granddaughter in her arms and began to tell her a story.

A Story from Tutu

The Healing Seaweed

KEALO TRAVELED TO THE BEACH NEARLY EVERY DAY to visit her beloved daughter, the shark, Kaleihepule. This continued even after Kaleihepule had been weaned from her milk.

Every day as she prepared to leave, her husband would ask her to stay home, but she refused. She was devoted to her child. Even though their gods had seen fit to grant their prayers and turn Kaleihepule into a shark, that did not diminish their love for that child one bit.

Every day as she prepared to leave, she packed food for her and for her child. Kaleihepule was a god and had already reached adulthood. Kealo would place the food in her basket made out of coconut fronds and she would head out from the mountainside of Anahulu toward the beach side of Anahulu.

As soon as she arrived, she called out a chant of welcome to her beloved daughter and rushed into the cool ocean to greet her. She did this for months. They would fish and catch turtle together. And at midday, Kealo would return home to do her chores. She was very careful to put all her energies into caring for her household and her husband's family lest her sisters-in-law complain that she was a horrible wife who could not take care of their brother. The community was quite small and peace had to be maintained at all costs.

One day, as Kealo was walking to the beach, she started to feel sluggish. She dismissed the feeling as the result of eating something that did not agree with her. However, this feeling came and went over the next month. When her menses did not arrive, she was overjoyed because she knew she was pregnant. She ate all the foods that her kahuna told her to eat and was sure to make all the correct offerings to her gods.

Kealo could feel the kicking of this child in her womb and even though she became bigger and bigger as the months passed, she could never rid herself of the nagging thought that she would lose this baby as well. It consumed her. It frightened her. It stopped her from appreciating the pregnancy. This was the case with Kealo.

She did not show this to her husband, nor did she dare show her feelings to her family or his. She simply continued to pray and hope that this child would live. And as the baby continued to grow inside of her and then kick within her, her fears gradually subsided. But, until she was able to see with her own eyes, she never fully believed that her baby would be healthy.

When her belly was full and it was obvious that she was ready to deliver, many people offered to help Kealo, but she refused all care. She did not want her husband. She did not want a midwife. She did not want any family to come near her.

She believed that if anything went wrong that there would be a chance that the gods would allow her to pray this baby into a shark as well. Her first wish was to have a healthy child. Her second wish was for the gods to show her favor again. She could not bring herself to think of any other scenarios: anything else would have caused her to cry.

Early one morning she felt the onset of the birthing pains. She started to make her way to the beach. Her husband was furious! He refused to let her go.

Kawanana had a mild temperament. Never in his married life had he ever told his wife what to do nor prevented her from doing anything that she wanted. Even if he protested, they both knew that it was futile: in the end, Kealo would do whatever she wanted to. This was no different.

Kealo stood up. Her back arched to compensate for the weight of her huge stomach. She placed her hand on her husband's cheek. "I love you, my companion in the cool wind of Kawailoa."

"My dearest wife, at least take some herbs that my sister has made for you." Kawanana opened his hand and placed the sachet of herbs in her open palm. Kealo smiled, turned toward the ocean, and began the long descent toward the shoreline.

The walk was hard but the distance was nothing because of the love that she had for this baby that she was carrying. She rested when she was tired, drank when thirsty, and walked when she was able to.

Just as Kealo reached the shoreline, she felt the familiar pains of childbirth tear through her. She put one hand under her stomach and lifted to alleviate the pressure. "A few moments, my precious one."

Kealo was comforted as the cool water hit her ankles and her toes pressed into the sand. Kaleihepule appeared just as the water came up to Kealo's thighs. Kealo let her knees buckle and fell gently into the ocean water as Kaleihepule darted around her in excitement.

I wish I could say that the baby came soon. I wish I could say that this birth came easier than the last one; but I cannot say these things. For all women, childbirth is not an easy process. They must bear all the pain and suffering that comes with bringing life into this world. For some women, giving birth is especially hard and they are lucky to escape with their lives and the lives of their children. Kealo was one of these types of women.

Kealo struggled in the water. She screamed and she cried. She massaged her stomach. She talked to her child and asked it to come out into the world. Nothing worked. No matter what Kealo did, her baby would not come.

Kealo was tired. She was willing to try anything. She reached into the small bags of herbs and emptied the contents into her gourd that was filled with cool water. "This will help me."

No sooner had she swirled around all the ingredients than Kaleihepule swam close and knocked the gourd out of Kealo's hands with her tail.

Kealo did not know the reason for her doing this. She did not understand what was going through the god's mind when she decided to do this. She simply understood that it is the will of the gods that certain things happen. If she questioned their motives, it was only because she was tired and forgot her place. Kealo accepted this action, leaned back, and let the saltwater lap at her temples.

Kaleihepule disappeared. Kealo searched the calm ocean water for her but her daughter was nowhere to be seen. Kealo was in such pain that she almost passed out when Kaleihepule appeared with some type of seaweed in her mouth and offered it to Kealo.

Kealo took the mouthful of seaweed. She started to cry as she chewed because she was deathly afraid that she would not be able to carry this child home to her husband. She was also so very tired and she thought that even if this child came, she would not be strong enough to help this newborn emerge.

The medicine worked. It worked right away. And the first thing that entered Kealo's thoughts was that she was going to make sure that this child was going to be knowledgeable in medicine. This child was going to ease the pain of other people. You see, even before this baby had even seen its first light of day, it already had a high expectation placed upon it. This baby was going to be a healer. And its knowledge was not going to be limited only to those medicines that come from the mountain, but would include those medicines that come from the ocean. This was placed on the child. It was right there even before it was born.

With one huge push, Kealo freed her child from her womb. The child was pushed out into the ocean water and so we say today that this birth was a sacred birth because it came out of one womb and into the womb of Hina, the salty womb, the ocean. It was born of woman and then born of a goddess. The child was still connected to the mother and it was Kaleihepule who cut the umbilical cord with her teeth and pushed the new infant into the arms of Kealo. Kealo lifted the baby out of the ocean and gently pushed its stomach so that it would breathe.

Her son's lungs pulled in the first breath of air. He was strong. He screamed to the world to let them know that he had arrived. Kealo held him to her breast and he began to drink. Kealo was so tired that she wanted to fall asleep, but she had to brace herself as another contraction brought forth the placenta. With her free hand, Kealo gathered the placenta and placed it in the gourd that she had carried from her home. She looked at her son. "We will take this to your father so that he may clean it and bury it."

Kaleihepule swam out into the shoals and found some fish that she chased onto the shore. She chased and chased more fish until there was almost more than Kealo could carry. "I will bring you some awa, my daughter," Kealo said as she threw the biggest fish to Kaleihepule, "but I must return home to show your brother to your father. I will return soon."

This was the remarkable birth of the son of Kealo and Kawanana. There was much pain and much worry, but in the end, faith and a belief in the people that Kealo loved the most brought her through.

Many good things came out of that day. Kealo had given birth to a beautiful healthy son. Kealo had pushed herself further than she thought that she could. Most of all, Kealo had sampled, firsthand, the potency of the medicine that comes from the ocean.

THERE IS A LESSON FOR US AS WELL: as bad as the pain gets and as hard as the lesson is, if we succeed, the reward will be great. We must pay attention and try our best and never give up. "Do you understand?" Tutu asked.

"Yes," Pua replied.

"Good," Tutu nodded. "Now, tell me what has been making you scream in your sleep for the last few weeks."

Pig Clouds

KAWANANA EMBRACED HIS SON AND SMELLED the top of his head. "My dearest wife, when I see you in a month we will have much to discuss," he added. "I am very angry with you."

"Yes, it was a mistake to go by myself," she replied. "I am sorry." Kawanana smiled, kissed his wife, and left the home to go to stay with his brother.

No sooner had he exited than fourteen female family members and neighbors descended on Kealo and her new son. "We must take care of you. You look dreadful," they teased Kealo, as they took the newborn from her arms.

The women huddled around Kealo and took off her clothes. Some started to wash her; some started to prepare a simple meal of fish, taro, and taro leaves. Some started to make a comfortable bed for Kealo while stuffing more dried leaves under her bed and scenting it with sandalwood. One woman pulled out a skirt made of fresh bark cloth while another took the gourd that lay by the bed in order to fetch clean water from the stream.

The flurry of activity embarrassed Kealo. She was not used to being waited on and even though she knew this is what the women of her community did, she felt uncomfortable. Many times when other women from her family and extended family gave birth, she was always the one that did the errands. But there was a side of her that was learning to appreciate all the attention: she was still very tired from giving birth.

She looked up and the women were smiling down at her. "You are so lucky," chided the elder Poluea. "Your son was born under Hikianalia—he will be wise. Hopefully, he will be smarter than his mother."

"Leave her alone, Poluea," chirped Pinea. "We can talk about that later."

Poluea clapped her hands in disapproval. "She was carrying a healer. The signs told us. The signs told her. The signs told her husband. How could you have been so reckless?" Poluea pointed.

Pinea stood between Poluea and Kealo's bed. "Leave, old woman, or I shall pull you out by your hair. It is not good to fight when the child's spirit is so weak," Pinea added. "Besides, what is it to you? This is not your house—even if you are the sister of Kawanana. Leave. Go grumble to your brother."

Poluea grunted, turned around, and stomped out the door. All the women turned and concentrated on removing the bad energy that Poluea had brought into the home. Soon they were busy cleaning and tending to Kealo and her newborn son.

"I will speak with her later," Kealo blurted.

"When you are ready to deal with her, you will," Pinea replied. "I will talk to Kawanana and make sure that he forbids her from coming into the house until the one month taboo is over and you and your son may come outside. Until then, we will all take care of you. If you are hungry or need water, let us know."

"Thank you." Kealo smiled at Pinea.

One of the women held the newborn to Kealo's breast and it began to drink. The slow, tugging motion started to make Kealo drowsy. Her eyelids started to fall and her body started to relax. "His name will be Kalau." As she uttered his name, she looked out through the open door and saw pig clouds sitting on the mountain. Tomorrow it is going to rain, she thought as she drifted off to sleep.

Muiona

KAWIKA LOOKED OUT THE WINDOW at the Keawe rain as the long drops slid down the faces of the leaves of the ti. He had listened to his sister's complaints for the last two hours. Ala complained that the lomilomi salmon was too salty at the funeral luncheon. She complained that their father did not love her. She complained that her father did not acknowledge her. She complained that he did not leave her any inheritance. She complained that the poi was too watery because their cousin, Kona, was too stingy. She complained that Kawika's son did not treat the aunties with enough respect. She complained that there might not have been enough opihi at the funeral luncheon. She complained that there should not have been alcohol at the funeral luncheon. She complained that the flight from Maui had been too expensive. She complained that Kawika's son picked on her son. She complained that it was too hot. She complained that too many people came to the luncheon. She complained that not enough people came to the funeral. She complained that the neighbors took advantage of Dad. She complained that there were not enough mangoes this season. She complained that the jalousies needed to be washed. She complained that the water was too rough for swimming. She complained that there was not enough seaweed. She complained that Oahu had too much traffic. She complained that the sink had too many dishes. She complained that Kawika had lost too much weight.

Without saying a word, Kawika stood up, put his jacket on, and went outside. He was so happy to see his sister. He did not realize how much he had missed her and her son. He made a promise to visit her more often in Maui. In spite of all the grumbling, he knew that she was just making sure that everything was perfect for their father's funeral and their father's burial.

She was getting ready to leave tomorrow and she was making sure that he would be okay after she left. He was glad that she was there to make sure things went smoothly. It had been a relief to just worry about preparing the food. He did not have to face all the family who came up to offer their condolences; Ala took care of that. He did not have to worry about the funeral arrangements; Ala took care of that. But as he walked toward the beach, he began to contemplate the new life that was before him.

On the path to the beach, his step quickened. Whenever he was troubled, he could always come to the ocean. He would let the salt water cover his entire body and when he emerged, he felt like a new person.

Kawika stood at the border of the ocean and chanted:

Greetings
O Kaleihepule, my companion!
A kahu calls, a beckon!
Waialua diverges into two,
Kaena has been burnt by the sun.
The sun, a sacred parrotfish flees,
the sun that paints everything a red color is setting.
Your kahu calls,
Come!

At the close of Kawika's chant, a dorsal fin appeared just beyond the rocky reef. Kawika swam out to meet his beloved Kaleihepule and hugged the shark close to him. "It is so good that you will always be there," he said as he rubbed Kaleihepule's rough skin.

Kawika went to the beach to look for the shell of a limpet or a piece of coral so he could scrape the barnacles off Kaleihepule's skin. After he had found one that he liked, he headed into the water and called Kaleihepule to come closer to shore.

As the shark came forward, Kawika could see something hanging from her mouth. The long, brownish-yellow object looked like a false koa: it was brownish yellow and seemed to be moving. As Kaleihepule got closer, Kawika could see that it was a huge muiona. It was dead.

Kawika pulled the muiona from the shark's mouth. He took it and placed it on the sand. It still had its color, so it had died recently. He was perplexed. What was the meaning of this sign from his god?

Rise of the Healers

PUA TOLD HER DREAM AS HONESTLY as she could. She told Tutu about the man and about the centipedes. Perhaps she had wanted to tell Tutu of the desire that filled her body every time she looked at the man who disembarked from the canoe, but she could not. This she kept to herself. Just as she kept the secret that she would trade a year of her life so that she could have her finger back. Even though she had lost her finger to a fish so many years ago, she still dreamed that it would make her complete.

Tutu was a healer. She was trained to understand hand movements, body gestures, and inflection in the voices of patients. She could tell as they neared her if they were suffering. Sometimes they walked toward her with a barely discernible limp. Sometimes they had a very minute impairment in their speech. Perhaps the color of their skin betrayed their health. Tutu looked for all of these signs to help diagnose her patients because at a very young age she had been trained to do these things. She recognized and understood the subtlest signs. It was therefore very hard to hide anything from Tutu. Her grandchildren knew this as well and had learned early on to give up telling lies.

But this time it was different. Tutu realized that Pua and Keola were no longer children and that she had to give them privacy. So, she did not push Pua. Pua would tell her everything when she was ready.

But there were some things that Tutu already knew about her favorite granddaughter. Tutu knew that every time Pua touched her hand and felt for the finger that was no longer there, she was hiding something. Tutu knew that every time she searched for that finger she was looking for something that would make her feel complete. She also knew that Pua was not telling her everything about her dreams. There was something else to this dream man. But it was better not to interpret a dream without knowing every component. One word or one gesture can completely reverse the meaning. Tutu understood this and decided to wait until Pua came forward with everything. Hopefully it would not be too long.

"Pua, go and call your cousin home to eat," Tutu said. "He has been at the Helekunihi home for a while now."

"Yes, Tutu." Pua stood up and left the old woman alone with her thoughts as she dissected the dream in every way she knew. Still, something eluded her, so she got up to make a late supper for her grandchildren.

As she baked a breadfruit, she recalled her favorite brother who was now in the spirit world. "Twin, I miss you. I must stop visiting you in the spirit world because my grandchildren need me here. I will visit you when I can."

PUA WALKED OUT OF THE LANE where they lived and took a left at the main road that split the town. She walked on the rocky path that bordered the semipaved street. Usually, she was nervous about running into one of the huge toads that littered the streets at night, but there was a full moon this evening so she could see very clearly ahead of her.

Her conversation with Tutu was still on her mind. The thought of having another dream about this man terrified her and excited her. She had never known any other love than that of her family and this was exciting. As she turned to enter the narrow pathway that led past a row of houses to the home of Mr. and Mrs. Helekunihi, she passed a row of white ginger stalks. She paused to smell some of the flowers and continued on to the home. As she neared, she could see the lights were still on. She walked up the five stairs to their front door. "Aloha," she called.

"Come inside," Mrs. Helekunihi called, as she suddenly appeared to open the screen door. "Did your grandmother ask you to fetch your cousin? He has been such a great help to my husband."

"Yes," Pua answered meekly. "I hope your husband feels . . ." Pua stopped. As she looked over the counter to Keola she could see that he was talking to a young man.

"This is my husband's coworker's son, Tiki," Mrs. Helekunihi said, introducing the two young adults. "This is Pua." Pua looked at the young man, who was the very same man in her dreams. Her face flushed. It got unbearably hot. She turned too fast and knocked some cans of sardines off the counter.

"I am so sorry," Pua offered.

"It is only canned food. Don't worry," Mrs. Helekunihi said as she picked up the cans from the floor. "Let's eat."

Pua wanted nothing more than to share a meal with this handsome man. She wanted to know everything about him. She especially wanted to know why he appeared in her dreams.

However, the only thing that came out of her mouth was, "I must be going. Tutu hasn't been feeling well since her brother passed away. She's cooking tonight, so I think it is better if we eat with her." She glanced quickly at Tiki's hands to make sure there were no centipedes attached to them.

"You are right," Keola agreed. "We were just talking about sports." Keola turned to Mr. Helekunihi. "Please stay off your leg for a few days and stop eating pork. Pork causes your gout."

Keola stood up to go. "Perhaps it would be good if you did not go anywhere for a couple of weeks. No phone. No car. No work."

"Yes, that's a good idea." Mrs. Helekunihi came from the kitchen with a jar of limu eleele and a bag of limu kohu. "This is for your grandmother. Please tell her to come by when she has time."

"This is too much," Keola protested. "Who is going to eat all this?"

"No, take it. Thank you for everything. Next time, you and Pua stay for dinner."

"Thank you." Keola kissed Mrs. Helekunihi on the cheek. "Please make sure Mr. Helekunihi takes it easy."

Keola said nothing. He walked silently back home. He was lost in his own thoughts and tonight he was a million miles away. As he helped more and more people, his confidence increased. And as he helped more people his ability to diagnose people improved. Mr. Helekunihi did have gout. The medicine that Keola gave him would help with that and get it under control.

WHEN KEOLA HAD ENTERED THEIR HOME, he could sense that there was tension. Mrs. Helekunihi's eyes were a little red when she had fetched Keola from his house—she had been crying. Another sign was that Mr. Helekunihi had a sore stomach. But a sore stomach is not a trait of gout.

Tutu taught Keola the importance of pinpointing the real source of an illness. Sometimes the illness was just a symptom of the real problem—a way that the body dealt with another issue such as stress, fatigue, jealousy, love, or anger. Mr. Helekunihi's stomach problem was tied to an emotional issue. The most important thing that Tutu had taught him was that kindness not wanted was unkindness. It was impossible to heal a person who did not want healing. Mr. Helekunihi had not asked for medicine for his stomach. He had merely revealed that his stomach was bothering him as a way of stopping the conversation that was occurring between him, his wife, and Tiki.

It was frustrating to stand by idly. Keola hated it. Mr. and Mrs. Helekunihi were longtime friends of his grandmother. Whatever was going on would need to be resolved soon before it really affected Mr. Helekunihi's health. Keola thought of the chant that Tutu had taught him:

Molokai is the sand; shells make this sand; rage is the illness—the calabash is the medicine.

Keola thought that perhaps he should mention something to Pua. She was on equal footing with Keola. In fact, she had an advantage: she was more compassionate than Keola and she had warmth that people liked.

Keola looked at his cousin. Her face comforted him. It was something that he knew and loved. He had known this face since the very first day that they were born. Now, under the Hoaka moon, he was glad that she was there by his side. They did not have to talk. They loved each other too much to burden this relationship with words.

As the two cousins walked home in the moonlight, Pua was lost in her own thoughts. Even though she pretended not to be interested in the young man at the Helekunihi home, she hoped that Keola would initiate a conversation about the young man from her dream. She was trying to remain calm but her insides were on fire. If Keola did not start talking soon she was going to bonk him on the head with the jar of limu eleele.

Their house appeared too fast for them: Keola enjoyed the walk while Pua wanted more information about Tiki. But as they neared the front porch, their thoughts turned to their beloved grandmother in the house. They could hear her shuffle with her in-house slippers on the wooden floors and the gentle clink of plates and glasses as she set the table.

"How are the Helekunihis?" Tutu asked. "Come in the house before the food gets cold."

Both of her grandchildren, glad at her recovery, entered the house, washed their face and hands, and sat at the table.

"I'll chop some of the limu kohu that Mrs. Helekunihi gave you to mix into the raw fish." Tutu rose from her seat.

"Tutu, everything smells delicious," Pua exclaimed.

"Is Mr. Helekunihi all right?" Tutu asked Keola.

"Yes. His gout is under control. I told him not to eat any more pork," Keola replied. "After we cover the poi, may I tell you about something that I think is making him sick?" he asked Tutu. "There was another person in the house," Keola continued. "I think that there is something bad going on."

Pua straightened and clenched the armrests of the dining room chair that she was sitting on.

Tutu replied, "Yes. Let's discuss it after we cover the poi. Eat. There is much to be thankful for."

"We are thankful for you, Tutu." Keola beamed. "Let's go visit Uncle Kawika tomorrow. Perhaps he would like some limu eleele," Keola said to no one in particular. He dug his spoon into the smooth poi made from piialii taro, took a huge spoonful, slid it into his mouth, and smacked his lips in appreciation.

Offering

IT HAD BEEN RAINING FOR TEN DAYS. Kealo covered Kalau's head
with a light kapa and brought him close to her so she could inhale his
scent. She had twenty more days to go before she could venture outside
the house. She had spent the last ten days talking to the two doctors,
her cousins, about medicine and healing. Neither of them was familiar
with the medicines that come from the ocean. Perhaps there were others
who used medicines from the ocean—how could there not be? But as
far as they knew, there were definitely none on this side of the island
and if there were any on the other side then they were rare.

When she told them how she had eaten a handful of seaweed that
had eased her labor, they became very interested. "I will find them out for
you," Kealo volunteered, "but I will need to learn more about medicine."

This new interest of hers made her excited and she started to be annoyed at the time that she had to stay in the house. She would never
dare complain about the taboos that her husband kept or the ones that
her family kept. She simply wished to be at the beach gathering seaweed. She was positive that there were many medicines that were un-
discovered. The thought of it made her giddy. But for now, it was better
to just wait patiently and enjoy this precious time with her son.

"I want to take you to see your sister, Kaleihepule," Kealo proposed.
"This is the longest time that I have ever been away from her. Your father
says she is agitated that I have been away from her for too long."

Suddenly, the door opened. "Who is agitated?" Pinea asked.

"It is nothing," Kealo explained. "Why are you out in this rain?"

Pinea took a step forward and held out her hands for her nephew. Pinea was Kealo's youngest sister. In their youth, Kealo took care of Pinea after both their parents died from smallpox. There was no love greater than the love that these sisters had for each other. This love was passed down to the son of Kealo whom Pinea loved more than her own life. She was amused at how this could be: how the arrival of a child could deepen one's capacity to love. She offered this oli to the little one:

> It is you my little one,
> little one of the verdant Paalaa uka,
> a mountain adorned with musk fern.
> It is for you, my calling, my affection,
> aloha that beckons like the fragrance of ginger,
> flowers with drops of dew,
> damp as a kiss on the cheek.
> Give me a kiss!
> A kiss for your mother.
> Let us share a breath.

Pinea started to cry, so great was her love for this child. Kalau looked up at his aunt and smiled. Pinea melted and vowed that she would raise this child as her own.

"Pinea, where is Kawanana?" Kealo questioned.

"He has gone to clean the taro irrigation ditches. He says he will return before the sun sets," Pinea replied.

"And what of Kaleihepule?" Kealo asked. "Has she been fed today?"

"Yes. I took awa this morning and offered her the ears from the dog that we cooked this morning. She is fine."

Kealo smiled. She was happy to see her sister and she was happy to hear that her beloved had been fed with offering, awa, and prayer. Giving dog's ears as an offering was especially thoughtful given their work this day. She placed her hand affectionately on the shoulder of her sister and squeezed gently. Together they looked at their infant, Kalau. "We must busy ourselves to straighten up this house before Uluhala comes." Kealo smiled. The two sisters placed their son on the bed and prepared the house to begin their fourth day of training in medicines and healing.

Soon, Kealo and Pinea heard a plea at the door:

CHAPTER 16

Beautiful Anahulu of the stalks of cane,
cane that is woven into hats like gossamer.
Here is the request,
may a path be cleared
for the voice which calls out.
Do not withhold the voice.

Kealo responded, thus—

Beautiful indeed is a hat made of sugar cane
but I have no need for this frivolous thing,
it is the warm bark cloth of Anahulu that I long for.
The rain of Anahulu is the Uailauae.
I was cold when you appeared.
Grant me your warmth!
Grant me your knowledge!
I have a desire for these things.
Welcome!

Kealo's answer greatly pleased Uluhala. It showed Uluhala that Kealo was serious about learning.

Uluhala entered the home and kissed the two sisters. She then walked over to the bed. "I am embarrassed that I have only brought my face today. Let me offer a prayer for this child as a gift."

After the prayer was done, Uluhala took a seat at the small table. "Today we will learn about the nature of man," she proclaimed. "It is important that you learn to look at people and begin to understand the reason they do certain things. Before you can heal anyone, you must correctly diagnose the illness. Sometimes what people say they are suffering from and what they are really suffering from are different."

ULUHALA TALKED INTO THE NIGHT. The only time the women stopped the lessons was to feed and change Kalau. Kealo and Pinea took in every word, every gesture. It was like being thirsty and finding a stream with cool water or eating the taro of Hanalei for the first time. This event moved their souls.

The Gift

PUA GOT UP EARLY TO DO HER NORMAL CHORES. She fed the chickens, collected the eggs, watered the plants, started a load of laundry, cleaned the bathroom, and started preparing breakfast. There was so much on her mind today and she appreciated her chores for occupying her mind. She put three eggs in the pot and lit the stove. She pulled out the jar of peanut butter from the cupboard and put it on the table before filling the coffee pot with water from the faucet and putting it on the stove. She could hear Tutu in the bathroom and could see Keola outside clipping back some of the plants. Pua exhaled loudly and shook her head back and forth; how was she going to broach the subject of Tiki without arousing the suspicions of Tutu or Keola? The coffee pot started to percolate so she took it off the stove and waited for the eggs to finish.

Keola cut back the chili pepper branches with the garden clippers. He was so tired this morning and did not feel like getting out of bed at all.

He was also burdened by what he had seen last night at the Helekunihi home. He had seen violence and tension in many homes, but this was different. There was something in that home that needed to be handled before it erupted. He was sure of it.

He had finished clipping the chili pepper branches, and started to weed the tomato plants when he heard Pua call him to breakfast. Usually he would be famished after taking care of the yard but he was not hungry this morning. He decided to go in and get some coffee.

CHAPTER 17

Tutu sat at the table and watched her two grandchildren. They were the reason that she got up in the morning. She knew them better than they knew themselves and this morning as she looked at the way that they were carrying themselves, she knew that something was bothering both of them. She did not want to take the initiative. They were trying to shield her because of her brother's death, and she loved them for that. She was also frustrated: she was stronger than that. How could her beloved grandchildren, who had lived with her all of their lives, not know her mettle? They moved around the kitchen believing that even the faintest noise would be a shock to her system and kill her. Ha! She grew increasingly annoyed the more she thought of it. Soon, all three of them were lost in their own thoughts.

Tutu composed herself and said, "Let me tell you the story of how Kealo and Pinea became the celebrated healers of Waialua and Koolauloa."

Tutu Tells a Story

The Celebrated Healers of Waialua

HEALERS NEVER EVER REACH A POINT where they know everything. They are constantly evolving their knowledge based on new information. They are constantly testing what they know to see if they can make it better, more efficient, and faster healing.

There is always room for improvement and so the greatest trait in a healer is curiosity. If healers have curiosity, they will enjoy reinventing themselves and their knowledge.

Kealo and Pinea were two such healers. The sisters enjoyed trying new things and they truly reveled in sharing this information with one another.

They were not sisters like Pelehonuamea and Namakaokahai, who constantly fought one another. These sisters were devoted and supportive to each other because they had been orphans from a young age. The silly things that so often occupy the minds of siblings, like jealousy or regret, did not burden them.

They worked side by side to make a living for themselves. If one of them had a sweet potato then it was understood that one half of that sweet potato belonged to the other sister.

So deep and abiding was their affection for each other that when Kealo was blessed with children, those children also belonged to Pinea.

And when their lives became consumed with learning medicine and Pinea wanted to dedicate her life to it, it was Kealo who asked her husband, Kawanana, to take Pinea as his second wife. Thus, the two sisters were not only sisters, but they were also punalua.

CHAPTER 18

They lived in the same house—without any of the bickering that burdens many homes. It was like this until the day that the last sister took her last breath in the waters of Anahulu as she swam with Kaleihepule.

The training of Kealo and Pinea took many, many years. It started when Kalau was only one week old and continued until the day that the bark cloth of Kane covered them. Their training took them to the various places on their island to learn the different varieties of all the plants they would need for healing as well as the zones where one could find these plants.

For years, they would learn how to use each plant, alone and in combination with other plants, as medicine. They learned what part of the plant to use as well as when it could be used. Some plants had more medicine in them at different times of the year and it was important to know when this was so the dosage could be changed.

They also learned how to repair bones that had been broken. They learned the structure of the entire body and how everything was connected. They learned how the blood flowed and how the heart pumped. They learned about the foods that should be eaten sparingly, like pork and guava seeds.

Their knowledge soon overtook the knowledge of their teachers. In spite of this, they were very humble. Kealo and Pinea were so humble that anyone from commoners to high chiefs could approach them. Everyone felt comfortable around them and that made them good healers.

Kealo and Pinea also had the aid of their child, Kaleihepule, who brought them different things from the shallows and depths of the ocean. The women would take these things and test them on themselves. Because of this, the women learned the healing properties of the pakuikui and the alaala hele and other things from the sea. This knowledge set them apart from other healers in the area.

Another thing that set them apart from many healers: Kealo and Pinea always shared their knowledge. Their home became a place for healers to come and discuss the intricacies of medicine and healing. Word of their skills and openness traveled to the other islands and healers from Kumukahi all the way to the cliffs of Paniau came to seek their advice.

Their discussions inspired new treatments and new ways of diagnosing the illnesses of the people of these islands. It was a time of hope. If there are secrets, then no one wins.

KEOLA AND PUA LOOKED AT EACH OTHER. It was clear that this story was a way for Tutu to express her feelings; she wanted answers.

Blood on His Hands

TUTU, PUA, AND KEOLA SAT AT THE KITCHEN TABLE. Each one of them was lost in his or her own thoughts. Just as Keola started to talk about his strange feeling while he was at the home of the Helekunihis, they heard a voice coming from the front of the house.

"Aloha," Pua called out, running to the door. When she opened the door, she was surprised to see Mrs. Helekunihi. "Aloha, nice to see you this morning."

"Aloha, Pua," said Mrs. Helekunihi. "Is your grandmother here?"

"Yes. Please come in."

Pua led Mrs. Helekunihi to the kitchen. "Let me pour you some coffee and bring you a plate so you can have breakfast with us," Pua offered.

"Oh, no thanks. I already had my coffee and breakfast." Mrs. Helekunihi gave the bag she was carrying to Pua. "These are mangoes from my yard."

"You didn't have to bring anything. Come, sit," beckoned Tutu. "How are you doing, Lovey?"

"Oh, I am A-okay," replied Mrs. Helekunihi. "Kale is good too—thanks to Keola. His gout is slowly going away."

"Wonderful!" Tutu exclaimed.

"Oh, dear. I forgot to bring the pie that I baked for you. How absentminded of me." Mrs. Helekunihi winced.

"Oh, Lovey, we don't need pie. Keep it for you folks," Tutu assured her.

"No. We already have one for ourselves," Mrs. Helekunihi said firmly. "I baked one just for you folks—special. I'll go get it and be right back." She got up to leave.

Keola turned around from drying the breakfast dishes. "No, I'll get it."

"We'll both go. I need to walk off that huge breakfast," Pua blurted.

"That would be fine. It is on the kitchen counter. Thank you." Mrs. Helekunihi looked at Tutu. "You have terrific grandchildren."

PUA AND KEOLA WALKED OUT THE DOOR to let the two women converse. As soon as they got to the front of the yard, Pua asked Keola, "What was that all about?"

"Don't know. But she did not want us to hear it," Keola added.

"Mrs. Helekunihi never forgets anything. She is sharper than a sea urchin." Pua giggled.

"I hope everything is good with Mr. Helekunihi," Keola said to Pua.

MRS. HELEKUNIHI LOOKED AT TUTU. "I think I will have some coffee."

"Yes. Let us talk. I feel like I haven't had a good talk with you in a long time." Tutu poured her dear friend a cup of coffee. "Is everything okay?"

Mrs. Helekunihi looked at the floorboards. "Kale said I am making something out of nothing. But I have just been getting this tightening feeling around my throat and my stomach has been so upset. Sometimes I cannot talk. And yesterday, I couldn't even eat, my stomach was so upset."

"Lovey, what is going on?" Tutu asked pointedly.

Mrs. Helekunihi looked at the floorboards again. She took a deep breath through her nose and exhaled in an exasperated manner out of her mouth.

"I WILL GO CHECK ON HIM when we arrive at his house." Keola really wanted to find out what was going on. He remembered the lesson that Tutu had taught him: kindness not wanted was unkindness. He would be careful before making a judgment or making a diagnosis.

CHAPTER 19

Pua did not hear a word her cousin said. And if she had begun paying attention, as she normally did, she would have seen the worry on
his face. However, she did neither of these things.

She was hoping that the handsome man who filled her dreams and
her thoughts was at the house so that she would be able to get to meet
him and talk to him. If she was just able to meet him then she was
sure that it would stop her from having the dreams again. The dream
would become real and would stop visiting her while she slept. This she
firmly believed.

When Pua and Keola got to the front door, they called out, "Aloha!
Anyone home?"

The screen door opened suddenly and slammed against the wooden
house.

"Sorry. Come inside," Tiki said.

When Pua and Keola approached, they saw that Tiki had blood on
his hands.

"What are you up to?" Keola asked.

"I am cooking. Come inside." Tiki held the door open with his feet
while the two cousins entered.

Lovey Helekunihi Tells a Story

The Curse of the Pig

TWO MONTHS AGO, KALE'S CLOSE FRIEND and coworker asked Kale if we would not mind watching his son for a few weeks.

His mother who lives on Maui—all his family supposedly lives on Maui—was ill, so he had to go see her. He didn't want to take Tiki because there is some trouble between the mother and the coworker over this boy. The boy's mother is from Tahiti and I guess she never got along with her. So terrible. So the coworker's mother does not acknowledge this boy as her grandson. I don't know how a grandmother can do that—just deny her own flesh and blood, but anyway, that's for them to decide.

Kale asked me if the boy could live with us. Of course, I agreed. I mean, we didn't know where this boy was going to go; it would be better if he just came to live with us.

Tiki is such a wonderful boy. He helps around the house. He takes out the garbage without anyone asking him. He washes the dishes. He even mows the lawn, which is good because Kale cannot do it now that his gout has come back. So, I really appreciated it. It is like we have a son in the house—only this one is better because he doesn't ask for money.

Last week we were eating dinner when we heard this knock at our door. It was our neighbor across the street, Mr. Keahi. I couldn't even see him in the dark, but he called out to me.

"Lovey," he said, "tell that boy to leave. He is going to bring trouble to you and your family."

"What?" I asked. "What did you say?"

"That boy is no good. He should not be in your house," Mr. Keahi said.

I told him to lower his voice.

"Why would you say something like that?" I asked. "That is not like you."

"You watch, Lovey. You don't do something now—you are going to regret it," Mr. Keahi said and then just like that, he was gone.

I turned around to go into the house and Tiki was standing right by the door. He had heard everything. I was so embarrassed. I felt so sorry for the boy. I mean, what could he have possibly done to Mr. Keahi to make him say such a horrible thing? I told Tiki, "Don't worry about him. He must be going senile." I couldn't think of anything to say that might make him feel better.

He looked across the street at the Keahi home. "Don't worry, I am not afraid of an old man like him. I can take care of myself." That's when my skin started to crawl. The way he said it was so calculated and cold. It was too many things going on and my head started to spin, so I told Tiki, "Let it go. Everything will be all right."

We went into the house and we finished dinner. Actually, he finished dinner because I could not eat anymore. Then we did the dishes, took a shower, and we all went to bed except for Tiki because he was watching television.

That night I was sleeping but I heard a noise outside that I thought was a dog. When I listened closer, it sounded like someone was making shi-shi outside. I thought, who is that making shi-shi in my yard? I got out of bed and I went to the window to look at what was going on outside my house.

When I looked out of my house, I couldn't believe what I saw. It was Tiki and he was urinating on my plants. Such a crazy night! Mr. Keahi and his weird accusations and then this boy making shi-shi on my plants in the middle of the night. I just went to bed. I didn't know why he was urinating in my yard. Maybe he was outside and just too lazy to come into the house or something. I didn't even want to think about it.

The next morning, I went outside to water the plants. I started on the other side by the kitchen because the sun hits that side first. I have all the white and yellow ginger on that side and the red ginger on the other side. I put the fragile ginger on the east side of the house so they get the morning sun and most of the time it is shade because they are not as sturdy as the red gingers that I have on the other side. I also have the guava tree on that side.

After I finished watering the gingers, I went to the back of the house and started to water all the plants that I have in the backyard. Mostly, there is all grass on that side but I do have all the potted flowers and vegetables. I gave them a lot of water because it has been a little hot here for the past few days.

When I got to the other side of the house, I was thinking to myself that I was going to shoot everything because I remembered that I saw Tiki making shi-shi on the plants. So, I didn't want it to smell so I started to really shoot down all the plants. When I got to this one part of the front wall, I noticed that there was something inside the actual garden portion where all the other plants were but it was kind of hidden by the red ginger plants. I pushed the red ginger plants over and do you know what I found? I found a tiki!

The tiki was of a man and it was about two feet high. I think it was made out of a hardwood. I didn't touch it. Who would put this kind of thing in my yard?

I called Kale at work but they said he was out in the field but they would leave a message. I didn't know what to do. Then I remembered that Tiki was there the night before so I wondered if he was the one who put that thing in my gingers. But he had gone to the beach.

I went into the house and I was so upset I couldn't eat. My whole day was wasted trying to figure out where that thing came from and who put it there.

I was inside the kitchen, just sitting down when I heard the outside shower turn on. I looked out the window and it was Tiki. I ran outside and I asked him, "Tiki, did you see the thing in the front by the red gingers?"

"Yes," he said, "I think Mr. Keahi put it there."

"Why would he do a thing like that?" I asked.

"I think he is trying to put a curse on me," Tiki said.

I almost fell down I was so shocked. Just then, Kale came pulling into the driveway. He wasn't even out of the car and I was opening the door to tell him what was going on. After I had explained everything, Kale started marching toward Mr. Keahi's house. Kale wasn't mad or anything. He just wanted to get to the bottom of things and find out what was going on. When he got to the house, he knocked on the door and Kama, Mr. Keahi's grandson, came out. We asked him to get his grandfather and when Mr. Keahi came out, he looked mad. His eyes were all red. He was sweating.

My husband said hello to him and he said hello back. Then my husband asked him if he knew anything about the tiki.

"I put it there to protect you and your wife," Mr. Keahi said. "There is something foul in your house. You should get rid of it."

My husband and I were worried. Everyone respects Mr. Keahi. So when he said that we were very worried.

"Tiki is my friend's son. He is only a young man. What could he do to us?" Kale asked Mr. Keahi. "Maybe this is going too far."

Mr. Keahi took a look at my husband and me. He shook his head slowly from side to side before looking straight at Tiki and then he walked into the house.

I told my husband that was so rude of him. We turned around and walked back to the house. I was trying to make sense of everything. I lifted my head up and I saw Tiki. What a look he had on his face. He was angry-angry. So, Kale told him not to worry. Maybe Mr. Keahi had something going on at home or something that was making him act this way.

Kale walked over to the tiki. He pushed the ginger aside and was going to pick the thing up when Tiki said, "Don't touch it. If you touch it, all the bad will attach itself to you. The only one who can remove it is the person that put it there." Then Tiki said, "I peed on it last night and I put Hawaiian salt around the house."

I know that I was working myself into a state of panic. I had a hard time to breathe. I felt a stone in my throat. I almost could not talk. And then I thought to myself, how does this boy know so much about these types of things?

And just as if Tiki read my mind he said, "My mother's family is from Tahiti. My mother and grandmother are healers and priests. She taught me how to protect myself." Tiki continued, "I also planted three elephant ear in the same garden bed as the ginger near the fence. I don't know how long he will leave that idol there."

I was furious. "Kale, you tell that man to come over and take that thing out of my yard right now!"

"Just let it go, Honey," he told me. "He thinks he's doing it for our own good. This will blow over soon." Kale walked into the house. Tiki walked into the house. I was still standing outside looking at this ugly thing. The more that I stared at it the madder I got. I told myself to just calm down and I went into the house.

About two days later, I came home from visiting my sister in Waialua. I told her everything and she invited me to come and stay at her house. She told me to plant ti leaf around the tiki but I told her that I did not want to go near it. Anyway, as I was walking up the lane to our house, I saw many cars. There were many people going in and out of Mr. Keahi's house. I do not know what was going on but there were a lot of people there. As I passed the red ginger in the front of the house, it just made me mad all over again to think that someone could put that kind of thing by my house.

Later, about ten at night, I was reading my book. Kale was watching television, and Tiki was in his room listening to the radio when we heard this lady kind of screaming in the front. But it wasn't like she was afraid or in pain: she wasn't screaming at the top of her lungs for help or anything. It just seemed like she was pleading with someone for something. I looked outside and Mr. Keahi's daughter, Kehau, was in the front of the yard with her son, Kama.

I was so shocked at what I saw. I turned and I told Kale, "Honey, come look at this right now!"

Kale came over and looked at Mr. Keahi's front yard. Kama was on all fours and he was eating the grass. He was acting like a pig and making pretend that he was eating the grass. He must be about twenty-two years old by now. Why was his mother carrying on like that? All of a sudden, this family was just going cuckoo. It was weird. Mr. Keahi came out and he was telling his grandson to get in the house. The grandson continued to roll around, rub his face into the dirt, and make pretend that he was a pig. Then the ambulance came.

They asked him to get into the ambulance. He made pretend that he did not understand them. When they tried to escort him into the ambulance, he bolted away and started to grunt even louder. This is all true. I saw it with my own eyes.

Kale and I went outside. We went to the gate and asked if everything was all right and if there was something that we could do. Mr. Keahi told us there was nothing to do.

That boy was wandering around so much. You know what they had to do? They grabbed him. The two ambulance drivers, Mr. Keahi, and the daughter grabbed Kama, tackled him to the ground, and dragged him into the ambulance. He was kicking and screaming like the Aoaoa wind of Mamala. It was terrible! I'm surprised that you couldn't hear it. He was screaming like a pig that just got its throat cut. What a racket! We just stared in disbelief.

This year, I turned seventy-four years old. I have never seen anything like that in my life. Even though I saw it with my own eyes, I still don't believe it. I mean, he was really crazy.

After the ambulance left, we turned to go back into the house. Tiki was sitting on the porch looking at what was going on. The porch light was on and I could see his face and I got chills all over the back of my neck and my arms. If I did not know that boy any better, I would say that he was gloating and was close to laughing at the entire situation. I told myself that I was seeing things and I followed Kale into the house. Tiki came in after us and I asked him if he knew anything about Kama. They are about the same age so I figured sometimes boys that age, they talk and they hang out with each other.

Tiki said that in a couple of days, Mr. Keahi would probably come and take away the tiki. When I asked him why he thought that, Tiki just said that he had a gut feeling. He went into his room and then he shut the door. That was that.

THE AMBULANCE WAS AT THE HOUSE ON TUESDAY. On Thursday, I was watering the red ginger and the tiki was gone. I knew Mr. Keahi had come to take it away but I thought it was because I had taken some fish over to the house; it was a goodwill gesture from a longtime neighbor.

My goodness, we have been neighbors for over forty-two years. Sometimes there are issues but we take care of it and move on. Kale said he thought Mr. Keahi was protecting us. This is a good thing, right? I just let it go. The tiki was gone. For whatever reason, it was gone. Fine. It was done.

Later on in the evening, Kale came home and I told him that the tiki was gone. Usually, Paalaa is mellow. In just this one week, there were a lot of things going on.

A few days after that I was washing the lunch dishes when I heard someone chanting at the door. I looked outside and it was Mr. Keahi. This is what he chanted:

> The floats of the sargassum drift in the bay of Kaiaka.
> A relish with the kernel of the candlenut,
> for Kaena is the poppy,
> for Puaena is the unicorn fish,
> for Kawailoa is the purple sweet potato,
> for Kapapailoa is the hard-shelled crab
> that crawls while his belly rubs against the sand.
> These things have been seen!
> A request!
> Grant me my request!

He took off his lei made of sargassum and he put it on the porch. He also left his bundle on the porch and he left. I went around the kitchen into the living room to go out to the front door. Tiki was standing at the front door of the porch.

"What is going on?" I asked. "Why is Mr. Keahi asking for forgiveness?"

"He feels guilty," Tiki said.

"Why is he asking you for forgiveness?" I questioned.

"Maybe not from me," Tiki added. "Maybe from you and Uncle Kale for the hurt he has caused you by putting that tiki in the front yard."

"Where is he now?" I asked.

"He went home," Tiki offered. "He will come back."

"Why do you think he will come back?"

"No one forgave him." Tiki said and shrugged.

I KNEW THIS WAS TRUE. I had not said anything because I was surprised to see him in our front yard. Kale was not home. I left the bundle on the porch and I went back in the house to finish washing the dishes and to wait for Kale to get done with work.

When Kale came home, I told him what happened. Kale decided to go to Mr. Keahi's house and talk to him. They were friends. In fact, they are distant cousins on his mother's side. Their family is of Anahulu for a long, long time. I think their great-grandmothers were sisters or something. They are family.

Kale walked over and he took the lei of sargassum and the bundle with him. Kale wanted him to know that there was no offense committed. He had no need to leave those things at the house.

Kale did not come back for two hours. He was gone that long. And when he came back, all he said was that he needed a beer.

When I asked him what happened at Mr. Keahi's house, Kale looked at the floor and didn't answer me.

"Kale, what happened?" I asked again. He didn't answer. He asked me for a beer. That is what gave him the gout. You know that Kale is not supposed to drink beer. I told him that he could not have any beer and he just ignored me. I told him that he was going to get gout. He didn't care. He had four beers and by the next day, he could barely walk. That is the reason that I came over to get you or Keola or Pua.

Last night after Keola and Pua left, Tiki went to take a walk on the beach. I was sitting on the sofa chair on the porch sipping some iced tea and Kale sat on the chair facing me. I could still see from his face that it hurt when he walked so I told him to not get up, but he insisted. I was so angry that he tried to force himself up. I told him to take it easy but he wouldn't listen. Then, everything just exploded. I just let him have it. It was all the stress and the anxiety and the anger. "What are you hiding from me?" I demanded. "Tell me what was wrong with Kama."

Kale sat back down and looked at me. "Mr. Keahi said that the doctors could not find out why Kama was acting like a pig." He looked across the street. "Mr. Keahi thinks that Tiki had something to do with it.

That's why he came the other day and apologized. He wanted to acknowledge that Tiki had stronger magic."

My skin started to crawl when I heard that. How could my husband listen to that kind of talk? I felt so sorry for Tiki. His mother isn't around. His father isn't around. He has no family at all on this island. And now we have a grown man picking on him and trying to turn us against him. I became even more upset. I told Kale that I was really sorry that Mr. Keahi's grandson was crazy. I was sorry about that because Kama is a nice man. He has always said hi to me. This is just ridiculous. I refuse to let Mr. Keahi blame Tiki for no reason at all. If he says anything like that again I will not forgive him.

I started to cry. I was saddened by everything that was taking place. I was sorry that Tiki's mother left him with his rotten father. I was sad that Tiki's father was a loser who had just left his son. I mean, I can see if he had to go to Maui for a few days but he went two months ago and we have not even heard from him. If I were going to be gone that long, I would have sent for my children. I would have called or written a letter but there has been nothing. He has abandoned that sweet boy. I was sad that even this boy's own grandmother does not acknowledge him. What a terrible, terrible family.

Kale and I looked at each other. I looked him right in the eyes and I told him, "Kale, if this continues, I am going to take Tiki and we are going to stay with my sister. You tell Mr. Keahi that he better change his ways. I mean it." Then I got up and sat next to Kale. "You better change too, Kale."

Kale looked at me, looked across the street at the Keahi household. Then all of a sudden the rain started to fall. It was the Keawe, the tentacle-rain. Kale and I just sat and watched as the large drops started to drip down the faces of the taro leaves.

A Gift of Flagtail

"WHY ARE YOUR HANDS SO BLOODY?" Pua asked Tiki.

"I'm cleaning flagtail." Tiki held one of the silver fish by the tail. "Can you guys stay for dinner?" Tiki looked at Pua.

"I don't think we can. Tutu is expecting us," Keola replied.

"I love flagtail," Pua interjected. "Keola, please tell Tutu that I will come home right after dinner." She walked over to the sink to wash her hands, "Let me help you cook these."

She looked around the kitchen for a dishtowel to wipe her hands but could not see one. "Tiki, where is there a dishtowel?"

"I don't know. I think Aunty Lovey put it in the laundry. I am wearing this clean shirt. Just dry your hands on my shirt—it's only water."

Pua laughed. "No, that's okay if they are wet. I'm only going to touch fish." But as she said that, it was obvious that he was interested in her as much as she was interested in him. She leaned over, grabbed a fish and a knife, and started to scrape off the shining silver scales.

Keola turned and tried to see past the doorway into the living room. "Where is Mr. Helekunihi?"

Tiki replied, "He is in the living room watching television. He would enjoy it if you went to see him." Keola leaped at the chance to get out of the kitchen. He walked in the direction of the living room. He paused, turned around to look at Pua and Tiki laughing, and then continued into the living room.

MR. HELEKUNIHI WAS WATCHING A JOHN WAYNE WESTERN. "Hi, Mr. Helekunihi," Keola said softly.

"Keola! Hi! How are you?" Mr. Helekunihi motioned to the couch. "Please have a seat."

"Thank you."

"My leg is better." Mr. Helekunihi beamed.

"Good. I just wanted to take a quick look and make sure."

"Yes." Mr. Helekunihi moved his foot toward Keola.

Keola looked at the foot. The color was normal. There was no swelling. And whenever he moved the foot, Mr. Helekunihi did not flinch in pain. "You can walk all the way to Wahiawa now, Mr. Helekunihi!" Both men laughed.

"Mr. Helekunihi, do you know my Aunt Nia, my mother's younger sister, and her son, Kahale?" Keola asked. "They used to live in Paalaa, but now they live in Honolulu."

"Yes, I knew them. Your aunts used to walk past our house on their way to school. That was a long time ago but I still remember them." Mr. Helekunihi smiled.

"I was just thinking about them because of the flagtail that Tiki is cooking. They had a big fight last year." Keola sat back on the couch, put his hands in his lap, and looked directly at Mr. Helekunihi. "It started from the party that we had for Tutu. You and Mrs. Helekunihi came to that party."

From the kitchen came laughter from Tiki and Pua and the sound of the hot oil as it crackled and hissed from the fish that were slowly lowered into the frying pan.

Keola Tells a Story to Kale Helekunihi

Burdened Is Kahale

LAST YEAR, AUNTY NIA AND HER TWO SISTERS decided to throw a birthday party for Tutu. They split the work between them: Aunt Nia would take care of the decorations, my mother would ask some of her cousins to play music and sing, and my other aunt would take care of the swipe. But all the family would take care of the food. They decided to make pork in the underground oven, taro paste, sweet potato, breadfruit, limpets, lobster, armored urchin, sea urchin, different types of fish, big-eyed scad steamed in ti leaf, coconut pudding, poke with seaweed, massaged bonefish, and parrotfish. It was going to be a feast and they were trying to make the best party that they possibly could for Tutu because everyone loved her.

I had a lot of fun making that party. I got to see all my family because we hardly ever have a time when all of us are all together. This time, we were all there. Our house was full with people. And there was always food cooking. Every day we went to the beach to go diving. Everyone was always busy running here and there to get this or get that. I was especially excited to see my mother and father and my younger brother. I never get to see them because they live in Honolulu. We were all together and everything was great.

One morning, Kahale complained of a sore throat and back. Tutu had left the house early that morning with the ladies to go to the reef to help pick seaweed so I looked at him. I looked in his throat but there was no redness. There were no white spots that would tell me it was thrush—even though he is too old to get it. I looked for everything, but I was unsuccessful. When Tutu came home, she looked at him. She did the same things that I did but she too found nothing. Then Pua went to talk to him. She put him into the room and she did not come out for over an hour. I was cleaning fish so I didn't really notice, but after I had cleaned a barrel of fish with my brother, I realized that Pua was still in the room with Kahale. But I didn't really think anything about it because Pua is more nurturing and compassionate.

After I took a shower to get the fish smell off me, I went in the room to check on my cousin. By that time, he had all of the aunts fawning over him. The weird thing is that my Aunt Nia was not there. My mother was not there either.

Aunt Nia is Kahale's mother. If her son was sick, why wasn't she taking care of him? The other surprising thing was that my mother was not there either. Kahale is my mother's favorite of all her nieces and nephews. He is my hanai brother. She raised him ever since he stopped being breastfed. She took him everywhere with her. But now she was nowhere to be found.

I peeked into the bedroom. Kahale was now in so much pain that he was crying. He did not have a fever but he was hot to the touch. I looked at Pua but she did not look up at me. Then Tutu came into the room and Kahale turned toward the wall. I got up, made a cool compress, and put it on his head. Pua continued to watch over him for the rest of the evening and Tutu made him some medicine.

Later that night, the men were outside cleaning the rocks for the underground oven while the women were outside cutting vegetables. My mother brought a pan of crab that needed to be salted. As she was about to rub some salt onto the crabs, my Aunt Nia grabbed her hand and asked her what she was doing. The crabs were already salty from living near the ocean; if more salt were placed on them they would be too salty and inedible. My mother pushed her hand away with force; it was obvious that she was angry.

"I have been doing this since before you were born," my mother proclaimed. "I know how to salt crab."

My Aunt Nia replied, "Yes, and every single time you prepare the crab, it is salty. That's why no one eats your crab. Stop putting salt in the crab."

We all looked around in shock. We were surprised at the way they were talking to each other. They were always very loving toward each other. We also couldn't believe that Aunty Nia would criticize my mother like that. It was not like her and it was disrespectful for her to do that to her older sister.

Tutu heard them and chided Aunty Nia, "Why don't you just tell her nicely? Why did you need to push her hand away?"

Aunt Nia responded, "I didn't want her to spoil the food."

Tutu, Pua, and I both knew there was something else bothering the women. It was probably linked to Kahale's illness.

Tutu asked us all to put away the food and to gather in the living room. She wanted to talk to us. We all knew that we had to make everything right with the family. There was no way we could continue to cook food if we were carrying ill will or hurt in our hearts: everyone would get sick if they ate the food that we prepared. While the family packed up all the food and went into the house, Tutu took a cleansing shower. Pua and I went to the garden and got some ti leaves and we entered the house.

Tutu had just finished taking a shower and was chanting a healing prayer.

She sat on the sofa and started to talk in a soft, loving voice. "I am so honored to have this family. My own daughters, grandchildren, sons-in-law, and cousins have all come to this house to prepare a feast for me. I cannot imagine the stress that you have gone through to make all of the arrangements. I also cannot imagine the amount of time and money that you have all put into this party and for that I am so grateful." She continued, "To me, this is the best part of the party—we have time to talk and reconnect. We have time to find out what everyone has been up to. And we get to comfort each other as we share our joys."

Tutu stopped as tears started to fall down her face. "I am so happy to see you all here. I am truly blessed."

She wiped her face with a handkerchief. "I know that each of you came with a big heart. Hearts that are filled with enough aloha to fill all the freshwater streams of Kane."

She turned and looked at my mother. "My eldest, I am so proud of you. I just wanted to say that. I am proud of you and I love you more than words."

Tutu turned to Aunt Nia. "And I am equally proud of you and the life that you have made for yourself. I love you more than words. I pray for you and think of you two every day because you have brought me such joy." Tutu walked over to the circle of ti leaves that we had made in the middle of the room and sat in the middle. She looked up at her two daughters and smiled. Then she turned toward my cousin, Kahale. "Sweet, handsome grandson." She smiled. "Tell me if your throat still hurts."

Kahale's voice cracked. He tried to push the words out of his mouth but they would not come. Tutu smiled. She turned toward my mother and asked her to start. My mother looked at Tutu. Then she looked away. When Tutu looked at Aunt Nia, Aunt Nia also looked away.

Tutu looked at the family. "I need to go to visit Mrs. Helekunihi." She stood and made her way out of the door.

When Tutu stepped outside, Pua approached the circle of ti leaves and sat. She looked at her aunts and her cousin. "Tutu knows this is about her and so she has decided to leave so that we may discuss this." Pua continued, "If possible, I would like us all to speak freely so that we may repair this harm and get back to the preparations of this party for the woman that we love more than words."

Kahale spoke with difficulty. He told the entire family of how his mother, Aunty Nia had mentioned to him that too much money was being spent on frivolous things. Aunty Nia did not mention this in an angry or mean way. It was just said because the costs were adding up: paper goods, favors, balloons, games for the children, flowers, limpets flown in from Molokai, and a new dress for Tutu. However, it was my mother Cupcake, Kahale's aunt who had purchased these things.

Kahale was distressed but, wanting to keep peace with the family, he told my mother that maybe it would be a good idea to cut back on some of the expenses. My mother became furious. She put everything down and went to look for Aunty Nia. When my mother asked Aunty Nia if she was upset because of the costs, Aunty Nia lied. She said that she was not upset. It made Kahale look like a fool. And now my mother thought that he had lied about everything that had been said. After Aunty Nia left, Kahale asked my mother why she had lied and she said it was because she knew that her sister would take it personally, and now was not the time to have a fight. My mother had let him be the scapegoat and his health had started to diminish soon after.

Pua turned toward my mother. "Aunty Cupcake, can you explain what you know to be true?"

My mother explained how she was in the process of shredding chicken for the chicken long rice when Kahale came over and told her that Aunty Nia was upset because the cost of everything was expensive. She wanted to talk to her sister face to face to find out the truth.

At that point, there were no hard feelings. She just didn't want there to be any arguments over the party because that would be bad luck. But when she was able to ask Nia what happened, Nia said there was no problem.

Cupcake became very angry with Kahale for making up such a silly lie. As she thought about it more, she began to realize that her sister probably had said that because Kahale would never tell her a lie. And if that was the case, then that meant that Nia had lied to her and that was even worse.

She had worked so hard for this party that she could not believe that her sister would not be honest enough to tell her the truth. Further, it was just a misunderstanding because most of the things had been donated. But she was still hurt that her sister had lied to her.

When Tutu called the family together to talk about the problems that they were having, Cupcake was disgusted and horrified that she would now have to explain everything to Tutu. How could she do that? How could she tell her own mother that her two daughters were fighting about *money* for her party? It was awful and shameful. Her face turned red. Cupcake was angry because she believed that her sister had ruined the party.

Pua turned toward Aunty Nia. "Is everything here the truth?" She asked, "What would you like to say, Aunty?"

Aunty Nia just looked at the ceiling. She began, "I have known my sister all my life. She is older than me so I know her very well." Aunty Nia looked at her sister and told her that everything that Kahale had said was true.

She did tell Kahale that there was too much money being spent on this party. She did tell Kahale to tell her sister. But she also knew that her sister would get angry. So she decided to deny everything and let her sister reflect on what was being said rather than kill the messenger.

She also knew that Cupcake would get angry with Kahale. How-ever, Cupcake could never stay angry with Kahale long because he was her adopted son. "But against me, Cupcake could hold a grudge for-ever." She stopped speaking and smiled at Kahale. "Sorry."

Pua took a deep breath. She looked around the room at all the family members who sat around patiently. The first thing that we must do, Pua thought, is to purge Kahale of his sickness. Then I will talk to the two sisters.

Pua left me to gather the medicine.

The family spent the next few hours gathering all the things they needed to heal Kahale. Pua prepared the medicine for him. He took it and then fell into a peaceful sleep. The medicine for the two sisters was different and more difficult to obtain because it represented years of misunderstandings. After the ceremonial foods had been eaten, the en-tire family, laughing and joking with each other, retired for the night.

When Tutu arrived home from visiting you and your wife, the first light of Kanehoalani's rays was already reaching the summit of Kaumeume.

When she entered the house, she saw her family sprawled out into every corner of the house. She checked in on Kahale and he was sleep-ing soundly. When she peeked into the room where her Nia was staying, she could see from the way that she was sleeping that Nia was having a restful sleep as well. When she went to check on Cupcake, who was sharing the same room with her, Cupcake was still up. Tutu asked, "Aue, how come you are still up?"

"I was just waiting for you, Mom," Cupcake replied. Tutu sat on the bed and smiled as the older daughter hugged her.

"Pua is a great healer like you, Mom." Cupcake beamed.

"Yes, it will help her in the challenges that she will soon face." Tutu said.

KEOLA LEANED BACK IN THE CHAIR. "I guess what I wanted to say was that there was so much miscommunication. If everyone had just come out with the truth, we could have avoided all those problems. Luckily, Tutu had a terrific party."

Keola leaned in toward Mr. Helekunihi. "There is a lesson to be learned there."

Mr. Helekunihi shifted in his seat. He was very close to discussing the conversation that he had with Mr. Keahi. Mr. Helekunihi wanted so dearly to talk about Mr. Keahi's son and his mental breakdown. He wanted so dearly to talk about Mr. Keahi and the warning that he had given him about Tiki. But there was no way the words could form in his mouth. There was no way that he could give voice to the ugly and terrifying things that Mr. Keahi had said to him because to do so would have been to give voice to evil and to call it forth.

Mr. Helekunihi was smart enough to know that Keola was suspicious of Tiki. To discuss anything about Tiki right now was to give Keola ammunition. Mr. Helekunihi did not want to do that. He did not want to hurt Tiki. Tiki had been hurt enough. He was just a young man. Mr. Helekunihi knew of the things that Tiki had been through. He knew the things that Tiki had suffered through. This was the reason that he had begged the boy's father to give Tiki to him and his barren wife. He had started to love this young man as his own son. He would protect him until the day he died. This is what fathers did for their sons.

Mr. Helekunihi looked at Keola and smiled. There was nothing that Keola could do or say that would make him reveal anything about Tiki. Tiki could discuss these things as he saw fit and in his own time. "That fish smells delicious." Mr. Helekunihi motioned with his right hand to the kitchen.

Keola knew that he was being excused. He also knew that Mr. Helekunihi was not going to reveal anything to him. He would try later. Instead he offered to fix him a plate of fried fish.

When he turned the corner of the living room that was connected to the kitchen, he saw Tiki and Pua. They were embracing each other and lost in a deep kiss. Keola took a step back and stared at the two of them. He could not believe his eyes. How could Pua be doing this? He tried to say something. He tried to yell at the two of them but all he could do was turn around and walk back into the living room.

"The fish is almost ready, Mr. Helekunihi." Keola sat on the overstuffed sofa and tried to smile. No matter how hard he tried, he could not bring himself to feel happy for his cousin. He just could not do it.

The Sea Spray of Puaena

PUA THOUGHT ABOUT TIKI CONSTANTLY. She was obsessed with him. She could not help it. She had known from the first time that she saw him that he would be in her life.

Pua had never had a boyfriend. This was all new to her. She did not trust these new feelings. She would have continued to admire him from afar because ever since she had lost her finger, she did not possess even the slightest bit of confidence.

The kiss in the kitchen haunted her but she knew that it was never going to happen again. Even if she wanted it, once he saw her hand, he was going to be disgusted and never talk to her again. So Pua thought it was better if she ignored him. She never returned any of his calls. Anytime that he came to visit, Pua made sure that she stayed in the house.

One day, Keola drove Tutu to see Cousin Kawika. As Keola started the car, he yelled out the window to Pua, "Someone is coming to get medicine. It is on the kitchen counter." Pua heard Keola but she was completely occupied with the task of peeling turmeric. When she heard a knock at the door, she pulled the cloth sack from the counter and headed toward the door. She was surprised to see that it was Tiki.

Pua pushed the medicine bag through the crack in the door. "Here you go. Bye."

Tiki did not know what he had done to her. He thought that she had enjoyed the kiss as much as he had. He could tell that she did not want him around her so he reached out to grab the medicine.

As he grabbed the cloth sack, he saw Pua's hand and noticed her missing finger. He grabbed her hand as she was handing him the medicine. "How did you get that?"

Pua pulled her hand away. She was embarrassed, hurt, and angry. Before she could answer, Tiki lifted his shirt and showed her a large scar on his right side. "I don't remember what happened because I was only four. My mother said that I was swimming and playing in the ocean in front of our house and something took a bite out of me. We never saw what it was but all of my family thinks that it was a shark." He traced the scar with his fingers.

She stepped closer and touched the scar with her palms. "I don't remember either. I was swimming and something bit my finger off."

"We were made for each other," Tiki proclaimed as he grabbed Pua's hand and gently opened her clenched fist. "We have been marked by the ocean." Pua relaxed her hand and let Tiki run his fingers along the length of her arm.

Her spirit had been stolen by the animal that bit off her finger. Tiki had given it back to her today. She opened the screen door and invited him in. They spoke until the Hua moon was on the horizon.

How could she tell this man that he had just released her from a burden that she had carried since she was a child? He had accepted her and connected to her in a way that no one had before.

From that day, all Pua wanted to do was to be with Tiki. She gave her entire soul to him and he gave his entire soul to her.

She tried very hard to do her chores. She tried very hard to pay attention to Tutu and to study her medicine. But she would just drift off and start thinking about Tiki.

As soon as she finished her chores, she would run over to the home of Mr. and Mrs. Helekunihi. Pua and Tiki would spend their days at the beach. Her deep tan revealed the hours that she spent in the foamy sea of Puaena. As it often does in love, her physicality began to change. Her hair was always a little wild. Her skirts began to become tighter around the hips. Her back straightened and she was always wearing a smile.

Tutu and Keola watched as Pua became mildly distracted. They were both happy for her. But when her plants started to get sick and die, Tutu put her foot down. It was unconscionable that a healer would not take care of her plants.

Tutu told Pua that medicine would be her first priority. If Pua could not focus on her plants then she could not focus on people. A distracted healer could kill by accident and Tutu was not going to allow that.

Pua told Tiki that she was not following through on her responsibilities. Tiki started to arrive early to do her chores for her. Tiki woke early every morning and did the chores for the Helekunihi household. Then while it was still dark, he would walk over to Pua's house.

First, he would start by feeding the chickens. He continued until all of Pua's chores were done with the exception of her plants. Those he did not touch: he was not trained. Sometimes, there were plants that had leaves that were rotted, but those were the very leaves that were used for medicine. Sometimes, Pua would pick the weeds that grew at the base of a tree. But it was not the tree that was medicinal; it was the plants that looked like weeds. It was very confusing and Tiki did not want the risk of hurting a plant or throwing the wrong kind of plant away. Besides, Pua said that she often spoke with her plants. Tiki did not want to get in the way of her training.

The ability to heal people is what had attracted him to her, so he wanted her to do the best that she could.

Tiki's relationship with Pua started to change him. Every morning as he set out to start her chores he thought of ways that he might get a job so that he could support Pua. Eventually, he wanted to have a family with her. He was sure of this. Pua was the woman who would share his joys and his sorrows. And he knew that it was going to take hard work in order to accomplish his goals.

Tiki read the paper every day to look in the classifieds for some kind of work that he could do. He knew it was going to be hard: he had no skills and he could not read very well. All he had was his two hands, a sharp mind, and the will to make a living for him and Pua.

Tiki also spoke to everyone he knew. He was always picking up odd jobs. He especially liked to take jobs where he could learn something from the other men on the team. He was like a sponge. He worked hard. Tiki began to make a name for himself as a hard-working, reliable young man.

When he had a job to do, he would wake up earlier than the colorful orange-crested roosters that perched in the mango tree in the neighbor's yard. He would brush his teeth, apply pomade to his hair, comb his hair, put on the clean shirt and pants that Pua had laundered for him, and head over to Pua's home to start on her chores.

After the chores, he would go into the house and have some breakfast that Pua had prepared for him. He did not remember the things that they talked about. Mostly they talked about dreams. But he did not dare allow himself to dream. He would plan out the things that he needed to do. He would work hard for them and make them become real, but he never wanted to look at those things as dreams.

Dreams were something that normal people had. Dreams were something that was given to people with normal families. Dreams were given to children by their parents along with hope and expectation.

Tiki's parents did not give him those things. Tiki's parents had not returned to claim him. They had not sent any letters. They had not called. They had simply ceased to believe that he was alive. Tiki was done with hope. He had moved on from hope and hopelessness. The only thing that was in his life now was Pua. And he wanted to offer Pua a life. He wanted to offer her a life that was real.

When breakfast was done he would walk to the street and wait for one of his coworkers to pick him up. But just as he walked out the door, he would turn to look at Pua.

Sometimes it was her long, black hair that he would stare at. Sometimes, the arch of her back, or he would just watch her wash the dishes as the morning light swam on her face. He thought about these things as he shoveled another mound of dirt or set another slab of concrete. It was the happiest that he had ever been and he never wanted it to end.

When Tiki finished work, he ran home, took a shower, cleaned the yard, took out the trash, and watered the plants before running over to Pua's house. Pua always waited for him. If it was too late in the afternoon, she begged Keola to visit her patients so that she could wait for Tiki.

As soon as she saw Tiki turn the corner and come around the house, it felt like her heart was going to burst. It was as if the whole day was divided not into hours or minutes but into moments when she was not with Tiki and moments when she was with Tiki.

If the weather was nice and it was not too cold, Tiki and Pua would go swimming in their favorite spot, Puaena. The sea spray of Puaena tickled their skin and brought big smiles to their faces.

After a particularly hot day, they decided to go swimming. Tiki was holding his breath and submerging his entire body under the surface of the water because he was fatigued after a day of working with concrete and lumber. The water was so refreshing. His favorite thing to do was to open his eyes under water and let the quiet calm him while the cool water removed the heat from his body. As he sat under the water, he saw a huge black torpedo coming straight for him. He knew from the size and shape that it was a shark. He bolted to the surface and began to scream and kick away from the shark. "Pua! Pua! Out of the water! Shark!"

Tiki scanned the area between him and the shore for Pua but he could not see her. It took him a split second to realize that she was probably behind him. She was in danger. He kicked his leg outward and turned around to look for Pua.

Pua treaded water and laughed her head off. She was laughing so hard that she almost drowned from not being able to keep her head out of the water.

"Pua! Pua! Hurry, swim toward me." Tiki panicked. He began to swim toward her. He knew that he was going to die but he swam as fast as he could. When he arrived where Pua was treading water, he tried to grab her and tow her in, but she pulled away from him. She was still laughing.

"This shark is my family. This is Kaleihepule." She pointed to the dark mass that started to circle around them. Pua reached in her swimsuit, pulled out a fish, and fed it to the shark.

"Where did you get that fish? Yuck!" Tiki laughed. "I've never seen a family shark before. I've heard of them, but I've never seen one."

"I brought the fish with me. I wanted the two of you to meet. Kaleihepule has been in my family since before I was born," Pua stated.

He looked at Pua and started to tear up. "I thought that thing was going to eat you," he confessed.

"But you came back for me. You were scared and you came back for me." Pua placed her hand on his cheek. "I am really sorry. I did not think that you were going to be scared."

"Why wouldn't I be scared if a shark swam up to me like that?" Tiki said. "I did not want to see you hurt!"

He had really been terrified.

Pua placed her hand on his shoulder. She tried to turn him toward her but he would not move so she swam around him. She could see that he was crying.

She swam closer to him. In a move that surprised them both, she kissed his chin. And then she kissed his cheek. And then she kissed his eyes. "I promise never to scare you again."

And it was there that Tiki professed his love for Pua. He knew he had these feelings. But he never knew the extent of these feelings. The shock of seeing the shark and the shock of almost losing the woman he loved were almost too much for him to handle.

He wanted to cry because he was so relieved. And he also wanted to yell at Pua for not telling him about Kaleihepule before they got into the water. But he realized that he was past that. He didn't want to dwell on fear.

He only wanted to be in this moment. He wanted this moment to continue forever.

All of a sudden, she felt something push hard into her side. It was Kaleihepule. "I think she does not want us to be together," Tiki said jokingly. "I have had enough of sharks for one day." Tiki headed for shore.

TIKI AND PUA TALKED INTO THE NIGHT about big things and about little things. Pua discussed medicine, patients, and people. Tiki talked about concrete, construction, and labor. The night seemed young and new. They almost forgot to eat because they were floating in their own time and space as the fragrance of jasmine drifted in from the west.

KEOLA HAD LEARNED TO APPRECIATE Tiki as much as Mr. and Mrs. Helekunihi did. Tiki was so helpful and he honestly cared for Tutu and Keola. Tiki was such a great help around the house that Keola and Tutu began to miss Tiki when he was not over.

When they had meals, there was always a place at the table set for Tiki. The only time that Tiki did not stay for dinner was on Sundays, because that was the day when Mr. and Mrs. Helekunihi prepared a large dinner for the family.

Tiki now contributed to the Helekunihi family expenses. He paid the electricity bill and the water bill. Mr. and Mrs. Helekunihi did not want to take his money. And they put up a fuss and a fight. But Tiki held firm. He argued that they still paid the mortgage. They still paid for all the food. If he was not allowed to pay for something then he was just a guest. And if he was a guest, then it was time for him to leave.

The Helekunihis could not bear the thought that Tiki would leave. They had come to depend on him. He was so thoughtful and considerate of their needs. He respected them. He coddled them. If there was something that needed to be repaired, he did not need to be asked. He just did it.

They had no idea why Tiki's parents had decided to just leave him. There were many people who would die to have a son like this. But they did not like to dwell on these things. It was enough to have Tiki in their lives.

In the beginning, they did not know how long that was going to be, but as time passed and there was no word from either parent, they just figured that Tiki would be there for as long as he wanted to. Besides, Tiki was old enough to make up his own mind. He was learning skills that would help him get a job. And most of all, he had a girlfriend that he adored. It did not seem like he was going anywhere.

Every Sunday, the three of them would gather. They invited Pua to dine with them and sometimes she came and the family would converse and talk into the night. However, normally, it was just the three of them. They knew that Tiki purposely asked Pua not to come so that they could have some time alone with Tiki. They could not say that they were disappointed; they loved all the attention that he lavished on them.

The dinners were calm and filled with loving banter. So calm that Mr. Helekunihi almost forgot the things that Mr. Keahi had said about Tiki. Almost.

Keola Begins His Journey

PRAYER HAS A REMARKABLE ABILITY to heal the body and the soul. Tutu taught Keola to integrate prayer into healing. She had learned this from her grandmother who was a healer. And her grandmother had learned this from her grandmother who was a healer. In fact, it was such a daily part of their lives that Keola did not see where prayer started and where prayer ended. It was just a way of communicating with the part of the world that was beyond what he had the ability to control.

His patients believed in prayer. Keola encouraged it. In the morning before they took the first medicine of the day—whether it was he, Tutu, or a foreign doctor—he asked them to say a prayer: "Thank your god for your medicine. Thank your medicine because it is giving you one more day to live." His patients listened to him. In some cases, their faith and hope was stronger than the medicine and Keola had witnessed its power.

Shortly after her brother's funeral, Tutu had become bedridden. There were even more chores to do. Her patients had to be seen. New patients had to be diagnosed. The plants had to be pruned. Food had to be prepared. Medicine had to be collected. Keola made visits to patients' homes. There were a lot of things to do, and barely a moment to rest.

Tutu was still grieving over the death of her brother. She was not a fragile woman but she had really taken the death of her brother very hard.

She visited Uncle Hanalei's son every other day. Sometimes even more frequently than that. Tutu liked to take naps in Uncle Hanalei's room. Sometimes she would be gone for hours and the cousins would debate whether that was healthy for her. It was strange to see her lying on her dead brother's bed. However, no one said anything out of respect for Tutu.

After a while she got her color back and she started to have a hearty appetite. She regained her lively step and felt good enough to see patients.

Every Hawaiian doctor knows that it is bad to see a patient if they are not well themselves. The patient already has a weakened system because of the illness. A sick doctor could not expose the patient to this negativity.

When Tutu was feeling better, she called Keola and Pua to her side. She looked at her two grandchildren and her eyes started to tear. "Aue, I am an old woman." Tutu smiled. "I need to talk to the both of you." She patted the cushions on either side of her. Her grandchildren sat at her side.

She continued, "It is time for the both of you to increase your knowledge." She paused. She looked at Keola and then she looked at Pua. "Keola, you will go first. Tomorrow, you will go to Waianae to a cousin of mine. You must prepare an offering. You will train under him—if he accepts you as his student. If he accepts you, you will stay with him."

She stopped and turned to Pua. "You will stay with me for now. Your training will be just as intense, but different."

Tutu got up from the chair. "This must be done," she said and walked into her room before closing the door on the stunned cousins.

Both cousins got up from the couch and looked at each other in disbelief. It was not unusual for Tutu to give directions without consulting them first. It was not unusual for Tutu to give them tasks. But this was the first time that Tutu had ever included another teacher in their training.

Pua was sad and happy that she was not chosen to go. There was a part of her that wanted to travel and to take on something new, but there was also a part of her that was frightened. She also did not want to leave Tiki. She cherished the time that she spent with him and she could not bear to spend even one day away from him.

Keola was happy that he could try something new. But he was worried for his grandmother and Pua. Since the day he and Pua were born and were given to his grandmother to raise, he had never been away from them for more than a few hours. He didn't like the idea that they would be at home by themselves.

Both cousins knew that Tutu had delivered her decree and it was final. There would be nothing that would change her mind.

KEOLA GOT UP EARLY WHILE it was still dark and did his chores. He prepared a small underground oven in the backyard. He began by placing newspapers that he had made into balls into a small pit. Then he placed small timber and branches on the newspapers. On the small branches, he placed medium-sized logs of kiawe wood. The smell that the kiawe wood gave off when burned smoked the meat and fish with an indescribably delicious taste.

On the logs of kiawe, Keola placed volcanic porous stones and lit the newspaper. When everything in the pit had burned and the rocks had turned bright red, Keola placed oilfish wrapped in ti leaves in a basket made of chicken wire. He covered the pit—now filled with fish, a chicken, and some breadfruit—with banana stumps and leaves to trap the smoke. He let the natural oven smoke the food for four hours.

As he took the banana stumps off of the oven, he could already smell the smoky flavor of the kiawe. He took everything out of the pit very carefully. He did not want dirt to get on the food. He put the smoked fish into a small container and took the chicken and breadfruit into the house.

He took a shower and got ready to leave the house. As he was leaving, Pua was just coming back from seeing a patient. "I am going to take Tutu to see Uncle Kawika," she said.

"Yes, I made some chicken and some breadfruit for them." Keola pointed to the wooden bowl on the kitchen table. "Please give them my aloha." Keola grabbed the fish and walked out the door. The cousins pressed their noses together and inhaled each other's breath. The honi stopped time and every moment they shared since their youth flashed in their thoughts. They pulled away from each other and Keola grabbed Pua's hand and kissed it. He got his things and drove to Waianae.

It took Keola almost two hours to drive to the other side of the island. When he arrived at the doctor's home, he was impressed with the thick Spanish moss that grew in potted plants that hung from the beams and the railings on the front porch. This was a sign of a true gardener because Spanish moss did not grow easily in Waianae. The plant liked cool, moist weather and it was hot here. As he looked around there were plants of all kinds: medicinal, fruit, ornamental, and flowering.

Keola approached the steps to the porch and chanted:

Kaala is the woman.
Kaala is the mountain that rises to the heavens.
Kalena is joined to Haleauau by Elou.
Kamaile is the plains.
Pokai is the Chiefly waters where sweet mullet are coveted by all.
Here is a house,
a house is lacking of comfort.
I call on one who has seen the sands of the eight islands!
To Niihau, of the light sands that get thrown by the wind.
To Kauai, of the white sands.
To Oahu, of the earth that smells of red clay.
To Molokai, of the shell-laden sand.
To Lanai, of the sand that blankets the peninsula.
To Kahoolawe, of the long sands.
To Maui, of the red sands.
To Hawaii of the black sands.
A reward is uncertain.
Come, let us travel together in the Kaiaulu.
There is only a voice.
A voice that calls out.
A stranger filled with aloha.
Grant me your affection.

Keola waited for an acknowledgment. He did not move. He focused all of his attention on the house. He turned his head so that his right ear was turned toward the front porch where he expected to hear a sound. But, nothing.

Keola realized that his first chant had failed to impress the occupant of the house. First, he had praised the land and surrounding features. Then he had praised the healing skills of the kahuna by recalling bits of an old chant that talked about how different illnesses were connected to different islands. To have seen the different islands was a metaphor for having mastered the curing of all these sicknesses.

Keola could do two things. He could do another chant or he could leave. But since Keola was not a quitter, he decided to chant.

Keola again faced the front door. He took a deep breath and intoned a chant he had learned from Tutu.

> Kaala stands in the calm.
> The large star has been placed on the long path
> by the child of the woman who beats a bark-cloth skirt,
> a skirt like the mountains before me.
> I am without a house, it has fallen in Luhi.
> The ridgepole is unsteady.
> The thatching has been undone by the Ahiu wind.
> There is no pili grass, no sennit.
> I seek a repose in Kamalu
> under the shade of a large tree.
> Grant me a ti leaf.
> A stalk from the line of healers and prophets.
> A stalk which was rooted in Tahiti.
> Spread its roots in Tahiti.
> Produced stalk in Tahiti.
> Budded in Tahiti.
> Blossomed in Tahiti.
> Produced in Tahiti.
> There is life!
> Life from Kane!
> Until my eyes are as bleary as a rat,
> until my skin is withered in old age,
> let there be some compassion for me.
> I am a man who is chilled by the cold.
> A man without a house.
> A voice asking for a teacher.

Grant me affection.
It is said, it is freed!

Keola stood in front of this house waiting for an answer. He made a mental checklist of the things that he had said in this chant.

He had praised this area of Waianae by talking about the majesty of the mountain of this area, Kaala. He also made a reference to the famous story of this area, Maui and his slowing of the sun so that his mother, Hina, had more time to pound her cloth.

He wanted the man in the house to know that he had bothered to do some research about this area even though he himself was not from here. He also gave the listener a reason for his visit: Keola was looking for a teacher. He was looking for someone who could repair a house. A man is a house and a house is a man. When a child is born, the parents cut his umbilical cord. When a house is born, the one who dwells in it will cut the umbilical cord of the house. A man will live inside a house. Just as there are things that exist in man. A man is a House of Wind because he has breath. Breath is wind. A man is a House of Fire because he has heat. If you put him under a blanket, the heat will come from his body. A man is a House of Water because he has tears, urine, and other liquids. When a man is unhealthy, he can no longer support these things. When a house is unhealthy, it will no longer be able to shelter its inhabitant.

Keola's description of the ti leaf from Tahiti was a reference to two things. He was commenting on the genealogy of knowledge that this healer had. This healer's knowledge was old.

The ti leaf is one of the most well-used plants. The plant is used for cooking. The plant is used in healing ceremonies. The plant is used for protection. The plant is eaten. The plant can be made into a drink. The plant is used as decoration. Keola had specifically chosen this plant to demonstrate his willingness to learn by referring to all the practical aspects of this plant.

Keola knew that healers of such renown rarely took students as old as Keola. Usually, students were chosen when they were young. The teacher would look for a child with special traits that other children did not possess. Some teachers looked for a child with a kind disposition. Others looked for children that were born during a special time of the year. Still others looked for children who were able to memorize lengthy protocols or chants.

Tutu had chosen Keola and Pua. She had chosen them the day they were born. He had heard this story a million times. Keola and Pua were born on the same day. As soon as Tutu saw them, she asked her daughters to let her raise these two children. "These are your children. These will always be your children," Tutu continued, "but let me raise them." The parents did not want to do this. These were the firstborn children for both sets of parents and their hearts were set on raising these children. So, they declined and took their children home. As soon as the children were separated, they started to cry. They did not stop crying. Then, according to the story that all the family tells over and over again at every party, Tutu took them into the ocean water and Keola and Pua stopped crying.

KEOLA LOOKED EAGERLY TOWARD THE HOUSE. Still, there was no answer. Keola realized that this was his last chance. The occupant of the house had refused him twice already. If Keola did not compose a good chant, his journey would have ended as soon as it began.

Keola looked into the sky and then he looked into the great ocean. He offered a silent prayer to his family gods. He prayed that they would communicate with him and give him the information that he needed in order to impress and appease the resident of this house.

He needed a haka to connect him to his spirits. He thought of haka and the portals that the haka could take him through. There were many portals into the dark place where the spirits live. The sun was a portal when it was at different places in the sky. There were different places in the ocean that were portals. Awa was a portal because after it was consumed, the person entered into another state of consciousness. It was in this state that the spirits communicated easily with the person who had drunk the awa. People who drool are also connected to that realm of consciousness.

Keola's family gods were the only ones who could help him. This healer was the real thing and Keola knew that he was demanding a chant that was worthy of his status. Keola was being tested already, and being accepted as this healer's student meant enough to him that he was going to use whatever tools he had to make a favorable impression.

Keola closed his eyes and thought of Kaleihepule. As her image entered his mind, he pressed himself even harder to remember every detail of this beautiful shark.

He pictured her long sleek body. He pictured the muscled body that tapered into her tail. He remembered her rough, waterproof skin. He remembered the spots on her head. He remembered the soft white of the underside of her body. As he started to visualize her, he pictured her swimming in the water. She was swimming toward him from the other side of the island where they lived. He felt her. She was coming.

Keola turned his mind's eye toward his other god, the bat named Uluhala. He started to picture the chubby, compact body of Uluhala. Uluhala was covered in reddish-tinged, brown fur. He called his god and the god came flying to him through the forest of Kaala.

The last god was the hardest one to call. It was the hardest to call because it was the god that was the closest to him. Keola closed his eyes and called the god named Poepoe. This was the god that Keola rarely called. It was the god Keola called when all hope was gone. The god he called when the soul of the patient who was lying before him was closer to death than to life.

Keola honored this god because he was his very own father who had died when Keola was eleven. And even though Poepoe had been gone for many years now, not a single day went by that Keola did not think about him. Keola excelled at healing because he wanted to make his father proud of him. In fact, Keola's moral compass was determined by his idea of what his father thought of certain things. If Keola believed that his father would disagree about some issue or about some course of action, then Keola moderated his behavior to comply. If Keola believed that his father did not like the way that Keola performed some task, then Keola would do it over again. Keola never questioned this instinct; he simply learned to use it as his personal guide.

Poepoe was a powerful family god. Upon his death, he had been deified by embalming his body in specially prepared and printed bark cloth. This metamorphosis mimicked the change that a caterpillar went through as it transfigured into a moth or butterfly. In the hoao ceremony, two people are wrapped in bark cloth in a symbolic gesture of becoming one person. Keola remembered as his grandmother and Uncle Hanalei, her twin, had prayed over the body of his father for days. They had never deified another person since then, and it was un-likely that Tutu would ever do it again as Uncle Hanalei had died.

Poepoe had the most powerful form that there was in the Hawaiian universe: he was a moth. His is a form that builds a house to completely change itself into something else. No other creature in the Hawaiian archipelago from the ancient times is able to do this. Even the beautiful parrotfish that uses its strong jaws to grind coral into sand and can change its sex, cannot change its shape.

Perhaps it is this power that made the ancestors say that moths were the food of lost, dead souls: by eating the moths, the souls hoped to be able to gain the moth's power and change into something else—someone who was alive.

Even those who grew sweet potatoes knew of the power of these formidable creatures with voracious appetites that could ravage entire crops in a few days.

Poepoe was made even stronger by his connection to Keola and to Tutu. Keola fed this god daily with chant and offerings and this is the reason that Poepoe answered his call.

This was the god that Keola called now. This was the god that he was asking to help him. Keola decided to use these three gods to access the other realm of consciousness where all sources of knowledge lie.

This realm is the dark night, the deep-dark night, the splitting-dark night, the black-void night, the deep night of the gods, the deep night of the foundations, the deep night of the stars that guide voyages, the source night, the heavenly dark night, and all the other names given to this realm. This realm was where there was no beginning and no end. All knowledge existed in this realm and Keola was accessing it now.

As his three family gods neared, each aligned themselves with each other and with Keola, east to west, to imitate the path of the sun. Keola waited until exactly half of the sun was merged into the ocean. And he began this chant:

A plea to Kanekapolei!
E Awakea, e Awalani.
The streaked halapepe, the yellow halapepe,
the halapepe that lies on the altar.

To Pohakea, I go
to build a house for Kane.
Kane of the lightning that touches the earth.
Kane of the stone is the foundation,
a foundation made of rocks.
The thatching is for Kane.
The projection near the top of the post for Kane.
The fork at the lower end of the rafter for Kane.
The gable for Kane.
The middle post at the end of the house for Kane.
The corners for Kane.
The lintels for Kane.
The end of a house for Kane.
The beam across the rafters for Kane.
The ridgepole for Kane.
The beam uniting the tops of the post for Kane.
The upper ridgepole for Kane.
The outside corners of the house for Kane.
The stone steps for Kane.
The end posts for Kane.
The sides for Kane.
Inside corners for Kane.
The upright posts for Kane.
The four corners for Kane.
The door sideposts for Kane.
The tie beam for Kane.
The trimmings for Kane.
The plate to fasten rafters for Kane.
The rafter for Kane.
The walls for Kane.
The entryway of Kane.
Eight garlands of foliage adorn the house.
A garland of ropes to tie the house.
This house of wind.
This house of water.
This house of fire.
This house for healing.

Inhabited by Kane and Kanaloa.
It is uttered!

By the time he was finished, the sun had already set. The last portal of the day had closed. His three family guardians were obscured by the dark.

Everything was still. There was neither breeze nor barking dog. The world had stilled itself in homage to the words that were in this chant.

Keola looked toward the house. Even though his chant had barely ended, he felt as though he had stood waiting for hours. Keola swallowed a huge breath of air and then exhaled. There was nothing else that he could do. He had just constructed the most potent prayer that he could.

Keola started to doubt himself and his abilities. He did not understand why it meant so much to him. It just did. He wanted to take his healing abilities to another level and this teacher was the one who could do it. Keola could feel it in his bones. And perhaps it meant even more that this teacher was making Keola work for just the opportunity to see him.

If he had invited Keola in after the first chant, it might have made Keola less passionate. Keola's desire to gain entrance was consuming him and making him dizzy.

Then he heard it. Keola cocked his head to one side so that his left ear was aimed at the house. A man's voice, brilliant and strong, chanted to Keola in the dusk:

For who is the beauty of Waianae?
The Koolau is obscured in the dusk.
But I am curious.
Let us eat until we are filled.
I am but a voice.
Come. Enter!

Keola smiled. He was grateful for the invitation to come into the house. He picked up the gifts that he had prepared and slowly made his way into the house.

As he neared the front porch, he uttered a soft thank you to the three family gods. Keola knew that this was the beginning of a new life for him. He also hoped to remember each step that he took now because they were the last things of his old life. Of this, he was certain.

Choices

THE OUTSIDE OF THE HOUSE was deceptive in its simplicity. As soon as Keola walked in, he was amazed.

The house looked larger on the inside than it did from the outside. The house was not cluttered, but books were everywhere: on the table, the chairs, the sofa, and the cabinets.

"Come this way." A man's voice called Keola toward the kitchen. There were pictures and paintings everywhere. It was a cozy home that gave Keola a warm feeling. It was if he had been here before.

"I have been waiting for you a long time to come to see me, Keola," the voice said.

"To come and see you?" Keola asked. "I am sorry but I just found out about you a short time ago from my grandmother."

"I saw you at Hanalei's funeral. You were very busy making preparations and cooking. The same healer trained us. Come closer to the light so I can see you."

Keola moved closed to the light. "I miss Uncle Hanalei." He could barely make out the shape that was sitting in the huge recliner, but from the outline of the shape, Keola knew that this was a small man. Maybe he was even fragile.

"Hanalei had many talents. I miss him too." The voice ordered, "Let me look at you. Explain your chants to me. What were you talking about?"

Keola fidgeted. Then he took a deep breath and started to explain. "In my first chant I wanted to praise you and your knowledge. These are the things that my Tutu has told me about you. She told me that you had traveled a lot and that you have seen a lot of things. She also said that your knowledge surpassed hers as well your teachers'. In the second chant, I talked about the sanctity of medicine. Medicine must be handled with care because the leaf contains the medicine to heal. The proper protocols must be made when picking medicine, growing medicine, handling medicine, and consuming medicine. The proper times must be observed and the proper protocols must be followed. And I know that your knowledge, as does that of my grandmother, comes from many generations. It comes from the primal source, Tahiti, and if that genealogy is to continue, then I needed to let you know that I wanted to learn everything that you are willing to teach me."

Keola paused. "When my three gods came to help and support me, I felt dizziness and started to chant. It was as if I had been taken to another place. A man's body is a house for his spirit. This prayer asked Kanekapolei to allow a person's spirit to go back into his body. The words came from my gods."

"You have the spirit world helping you. That is good. Very good."

Keola bent his head down in gratitude.

"Why should I take you as a student? What can you offer?" the voice asked.

Keola paused and looked at the floor. "I cannot answer that because I cannot give words to something that is there but has no name. My desire to learn, to teach, and most of all, to heal are the things that make me get up in the morning. I am consumed by medicine and the ability to help people.

"Come closer," the voice instructed. "I want you to see me."

Keola moved closer. As he moved, the light that was emanating from behind him was allowed to shine on the recliner where the voice was coming from. He saw that a pitiful form—indeed, a man without any arms or legs—hosted the voice.

"Does my appearance scare you?"

"No," Keola responded. "In fact, it inspires me that even though you have no arms or legs that you have become one of the most renowned healers in Hawaii."

"My cousin has taught you well. She did good to send you to me. And I am ready to accept a new student as the other has learned all that

I can teach." The voice continued, "You will call me Kumu. I did not have the time to visit with you at Hanalei's funeral. I had a patient who was dying and could not visit with the family." He paused for a second. "Where are your things?"

"In the car, Kumu."

"Bring them in the house. You must be tired. You may take a shower and then we eat together. Your bedroom is the first room on the left. Mine is the one next to the kitchen. We start with your training to-morrow. We will telephone my cousin to let her know that you will be staying here."

Keola went to the car and got his things. How is it that he never remembered meeting this man? Things were so confusing at Uncle Hanalei's funeral and Keola had been occupied but it was odd that he did not remember meeting or even hearing about this man. It was not like his arrival would have gone unnoticed. He had a strong bearing, in addition to his unique physical shape.

Before he went back into the house he offered his gods a prayer of thanks. As he looked up into the sky he noticed the moon. It was Hua.

26

Pua Makes a Decision

PUA WAS HEARTBROKEN THAT HER COUSIN WAS GONE. She thought about him every second of the day. They had lived together ever since they were born and she was not coping well. She was quick tempered. She was irritable. And she was losing focus in her training.

Unfortunately for Tiki, most of her anger was directed at him. Nothing he did was right. He did not cook their meals the right way. He did not mow the lawn the correct way. And he did not feed the animals the correct way. Everything he did was wrong. And Pua lashed out at him.

Tiki decided to spend a little time away from Pua in order to give her the space she needed. But as soon as he did that, she blamed him for abandoning her. She accused him of not loving her. She accused him of finding someone else. Whatever he did he could not win.

Tiki was very confused. He wanted to talk to Tutu about it but she was so consumed with training Pua and picking up the slack from Keola's absence that he did not want to burden her with his relationship problems. He also did not want to go to Mr. and Mrs. Helekunihi to ask advice because they thought that Pua and Tiki were the perfect couple and he did not want them to think harshly of Pua. But each day, the anger and the fighting became more and more frequent. Tiki felt like he was going to explode.

Early Sunday morning as Tiki was feeding the chickens, Pua came to the chicken coop and started to scold Tiki for not properly closing the trash can filled with chicken seed. "The ants will get in and then it

109

will get moldy," Pua scolded him. "Why can't you do anything right? Must I be your parent too? No wonder they left you."

It had been uttered. Pua had said to Tiki the one thing that made his issues surface. His parents' abandonment of him. He tried to contain his rage. He really tried to remember that he loved this woman. He tried to remember all the cherished times with her. But nothing helped. He took the pail that contained the chicken seed and smashed it into her head.

The impact of the blow made her stagger back. Pua could not contain her shock. Her eyes bulged out of her head in disbelief at what had just happened. She fell back into the small pails of slop that contained all the slop for the pigs and rolled into the cherry tomato plants. And as soon as she saw the blood that dripped from her forehead, she started to cry.

Tiki could not believe what he had just done. He ran over to Pua and tried to help her up, but she screamed for him to stay away from her. No matter what he did, he could not appease her. In one quick instant, their entire relationship was reduced to fear and anger.

Tiki begged and pleaded but the damage was done. Pua ran into the house and locked the door. Tiki pounded on the door. "Pua, let me in." But there was no response. Tiki pounded on the door again. "Honey, I am so sorry. I did not mean to hurt you. You are the best thing in my life." But she would not open the door. Tiki slumped into the wooden door and stayed there for hours until Tutu came home from visiting Kawika.

"Tiki, what are you doing outside? It is so late. Why are you not in the house?"

Tiki did not have the courage or the strength to face her. He picked himself up and walked home without saying a word.

Tutu opened the door and went in. The interior of the house was dark. "Pua?" she called. But there was no answer.

Tutu had a strange feeling that something was wrong so she headed in the direction of Pua's room. The door was closed. She knocked on it three times and even though she did not hear an answer, she walked in. From the doorway, she could see that Pua was sleeping. She walked in and listened to the steady rhythm of her breathing. She took a blanket and covered her granddaughter with it, left the room, and shut the door behind her.

What she could not see was that Pua's forehead was still matted with blood.

Pua had fallen asleep crying. Sleep did not offer her any comfort. Her dreams were of centipedes.

PUA HAD NOT DREAMED OF CENTIPEDES for almost a year. But this dream was as vivid as it was terrible. Again, she made out the appearance of a man sitting in a canoe. He was paddling the canoe very gently with his oars barely skimming the face of the calm ocean water. In the second seat of the canoe, she could make out the figure of an old man who was carrying a basket woven from coconut fronds. The old man remained seated in the canoe. The young man jumped out of the canoe and onto the sand. The young, handsome man neared Pua and reached out to touch her face. His hand was a long whip of centipedes that stung her face again and again. They separated her eyeballs from their sockets and crawled into them. She felt the tiny legs dig their way into her soft, internal flesh. They crawled into her nose, ears, and mouth. They crawled into her throat and wriggled into her belly where they stung her over and over again. They crawled in between the vertebrae of her spine. The stingers of the centipedes lashed her a thousand times inside of her body. She screamed in pain.

The young man was Tiki. Tiki was the man whose hands were made of centipedes. Pua screamed and awoke. She was flushed and her entire body felt as though someone had poked her with a thousand needles.

Pua felt her forehead. The dried blood was still matted to her hair. She got up slowly and made her way across the room. She opened her bedroom door and looked around to make sure that Tutu was not in the hallway. She quickly walked into the bathroom and shut the door behind her. She walked over to the mirror and looked at her reflection. She gasped when she saw the gash in her forehead and the large lump.

She turned the warm water on and started to wash her face. The memory of what had happened the night before weighed heavily. She felt betrayed and hurt. She was the one who had said that horrible thing about Tiki's parents abandoning him. She was the one who did not appreciate how hard he had worked for her and Tutu ever since Keola went to live on the other side of the island. Worse, how was she going to explain the gash on her forehead to Tutu?

Pua took a shower. When she got out, she carefully arranged her hair to give her bangs so that she could cover the gash. She went into the kitchen to prepare breakfast. When she walked into the kitchen, she saw Tiki, and took a step back.

"I am so sorry." Tiki fell to the floor and embraced her legs. "You are the world to me. You are my life. I don't know what came over me." He squeezed her legs and tried to hold on to her for dear life.

"Get up before Tutu comes in and sees us," Pua said frantically.

"I don't care if she sees us. I want her to know how sorry I am."

"She doesn't know. Get up." Pua lifted him up. "We will talk about this later." She opened the refrigerator and took out some eggs. "Can you please make some hot water for the coffee?" she asked Tiki.

He almost ran to where the pot was. He took it out and filled it with water from the tap. He weighed the correct amount of coffee, put it in the percolator, and plugged the unit into the electrical socket.

Tutu entered the kitchen just as breakfast was done cooking. "Good morning, my loves," she beamed. "What a fantastic morning."

Tiki and Pua looked outside, their thoughts a million miles from each other.

Tutu sat down at her place at the table. She knew that something was not right this morning, but she decided that they needed to work out their own differences. They had been dating for over a year now and she needed to stay out of their business. They were old enough. Pua had been so irritable lately. Tutu pitied her. She knew that Pua missed Keola dearly. She also knew that the new training was stressing Pua out. But Tutu also knew that Pua was pregnant. She wondered if Pua knew that this was the real reason why she was nervous and irritable. Pua was suffering from chemical imbalance from her pregnancy.

Everyone ate breakfast in silence although Tutu was cheery. This was going to be her first great-grandchild. She would welcome this baby with all the joy and love that she had in her heart.

As soon as she was done with her light breakfast of eggs, toast, coffee, and some fried fish, Tutu went into the garden to care for her plants.

Pua and Tiki got up to wash the dishes.

"Can we talk about this?" Tiki asked Pua.

"Tiki, you hit me," Pua said, spitting out the words.

"I don't know what came over me. I will never hurt you again," Tiki pleaded.

"I want you to get out of this house. I want you to leave. I don't want you to come back, ever." Pua looked him in his eyes. "We are over."

Tiki started to weep.

"Get out right now. Before I scream," Pua threatened. "Get out of here right now and don't come back."

"I can't let you go. I am sorry," Tiki pleaded.

"If you care for me as much as you say, then you will listen to me now. Do not come over again until I call you back." She turned. "If I call you back." She left the kitchen.

Tiki looked around. He wondered if he should plead his case again. He wondered if he should talk to Tutu. He wondered if he should just walk out into the yard and complete his chores like he would normally do. He wanted to take this house apart. He wanted to rip the sink out. He wanted to smash holes in the wall with his fists. He wanted to kick all the cupboards in.

How could he have been so stupid? How could he have let his rage take control of him? He had been so good. He had kept it under control. Now everyone would know. He would lose the woman he loved. He would lose his new family.

In a moment of clarity, Tiki left Tutu's home. He took a walk and went to the beach. He jumped in the water, let a hundred cold waves lap over him until he was calm and could face what lay in store for him. He wasn't ready to give up on his relationship with Pua. He was going to fight his anger and show Pua the kind of man and husband that he could be. He had no choice; he loved her with all his heart. And he had nowhere else to go.

The Sickness of Ahi

FIRST, AHI TOLD HIMSELF THAT THESE SIGNS were not anything serious, that they were natural progressions of age. Then the worry started to set in after his conditions worsened. In fact, worry and darkness started to set in as he noticed that with each day that he left himself unchecked, a new, more insidious symptom arrived. And with each week that passed, there was one less thing that he could do.

First, it was hard for him to dive to a certain depth. He could do it before, but then it got harder and harder to hold his breath. Then it was hard for him to get to the beach because he could barely walk across the open field that stood between his house and the water.

Finally, he could not even walk to the car without being in horrible pain. His legs felt like buckling halfway to his car.

Ahi hid his illness for a while. It had started with fatigue. He was always tired. But he figured it was because he was working too hard. So he varied the medicine that he was taking. When the fatigue did not go away, he changed his medicine. He also prayed more.

When the herbs that he was taking were failing to help his fatigue, he tried other medicines. He was still tired but he attributed that to the death of an uncle. There were a lot of things to do then. There were arrangements to make and family to console. There was food to be cooked, and his cousins had relied heavily on Ahi to make sure those things went smoothly. It had been an exhausting time and he attributed his fatigue to that.

Ahi became even more fatigued. Except he knew by this time that there was more to it than just simple tiredness. When Ahi got his first fever, he thought it was because he had stayed out too late in the cold Hapaiwai wind of Paalaa. It is a chilly wind that blows from the north and carries moisture that goes right through clothes. The fever only lasted a day but two weeks later it was back and it lasted for two days.

Pain and weight loss alarmed Ahi. Pains right below his ribs caused Ahi to lose his appetite. When he started to rapidly lose weight he started to worry. Ahi had never lost so much weight in such a short time. He had not wanted to alarm the family but he knew that something was happening to his body. There were things that started to occur after the weight loss. He started to bruise easily. When he hit his arm on the refrigerator door, his arm had a dark bruise. When Ahi's son sat on his lap, he developed a large bruise. This was not normal. But Ahi had never seen this type of illness before. And he was very worried.

When Ahi arrived at Kumu's home, he was weak and ill.

While Ahi waited in the living room, Kumu looked at Keola. "You will watch what I do. If I need something you will get it. You will be my arms and my legs. You will not ask questions while the patient is here. You will not make any face that shows pity, disgust, or surprise, or any nature of things that might lead the patient into believing something that I do not want them to. You will not even talk to the patient—even if they ask you a question directly. These are the conditions of you training with me. If you cannot do any of these things then you may return to your grandmother."

"I will do everything you ask, Kumu," Keola replied.

Ahi's decision not to seek medical care sooner was a grave mistake. Keola saw this error more often than he would have liked to. Perhaps it was the inability of people to confront their mortality. Perhaps it was the belief that people have in their self-healing abilities. Perhaps people did not like to face the truth because they hated to go to the doctors or the hospital. Whatever the reason, it was dangerous.

Kumu wanted Keola to remember that each patient was an individual who feared, loved, thrived, and got sick. It was up to the healer to find that motivation that would help the patient recover and recover quickly. Being in touch with the mind of the patient was the first step to prescribing a healthy cure. If a patient could not imagine his wellness, then all was lost. There had to be a goal that the patient strived for. Only then would he want to be healed.

Kumu got to work on examining Ahi.

"Keola, feel his pulse. Does his heart beat regularly?"

"Keola, listen to his breath. Is it labored?"

"Keola, look at his urine. Is it cloudy? Orange?"

The questions continued until everything had been checked. One answer led to another set of questions. Each question focused on the cause of the sickness that was plaguing the patient.

Keola acted as the hands for Kumu. He gently touched and prodded the patient under the specific directions and complete supervision of Kumu.

Kumu asked Ahi many questions: "How is your family? How is your wife? How are your children? How is your sister?"

After hours of observation and discussion, Kumu told Ahi, "You will sleep here tonight. Go, rest. We will call you when dinner is ready."

"Is it bad?" Ahi asked.

"We do not know yet," Kumu replied. "We will do everything we can."

Keola led Ahi into the guest bedroom. Ahi was exhausted and immediately he fell into a deep sleep. Keola took out Ahi's clothes from the suitcase and arranged them nicely in the dresser drawers.

Keola went into the kitchen to prepare a simple dinner of taro tops and fish for the three of them. As soon as it was done, he told Kumu.

"Take me to the table. But do not bother Ahi," Kumu told Keola.

"His sickness is bad?" Keola asked.

"Yes. He will be dead by tomorrow morning," Kumu replied. "He was already taking medicine from another doctor. And he lost faith in the doctor and the medicine." Kumu paused for two seconds. "He took so long to come to see me because he did not want to survive. His symptoms were already so horrible that he could barely stand."

Keola looked at Kumu in disbelief. "But don't we want to save people?"

"We cannot save those that do not want to be saved." Kumu leaned forward to look at the scrumptious taro and fish. "Kindness not wanted is unkindness." Keola had heard his grandmother say that very same thing.

"The very first thing that you must remember about healing is that it is never up to you. The patient decides if they are going to be healed. The patient decides if they are going to die," Kumu offered.

"But isn't there anything in all those books that you have that can give us a clue how to help him?" Keola asked.

"Those books are not books about medicine," Kumu answered. "Those books are about culture and art and literature. They help me look into the mind of my patients. Everything I learned about medicine I learned from my teachers and from practicing," Kumu said patiently. "Those books help me understand why people make the decisions they do— even if those decisions are bad for them." Kumu looked at the food on the table. "Let's eat. Tomorrow, we will call Ahi's family."

Keola bowed his head in agreement. He grabbed a spoon, scooped up some of the hot taro tops, and blew on it before feeding it to his teacher.

Kumu looked up. "This is delicious. Just what we needed on a night like this."

Keola scooped another spoonful for Kumu. This was not what he expected.

AFTER THE MEAL, KEOLA TOOK KUMU into the living room and went back into the kitchen to wash the dishes.

When he was done with the dishes, he gave Kumu a bath in warm water that was perfumed with sandalwood.

"Tonight we will talk about the nature of Hawaiians," Kumu said. "Take a shower and meet me in the living room."

Keola took a shower and let the cold water run over him. It was hard to accept that he could not heal Ahi.

Keola had enough medical training to know that there was always a reason for something. Even though he had doubts that Ahi was beyond cure, he would never go against Kumu.

Kumu was a celebrated healer and knew more than Keola could ever hope to know. So he resigned himself to his teacher's assessment.

After he was done taking a shower, he dressed and went into the living room.

Kumu was sitting on the sofa. "Keola, on the top of that cupboard is a heavy box that contains stones. Bring it down and take the stones out."

A Map of Man

KEOLA TOOK THE STONES OUT OF THE BOX and laid them out according to Kumu's directions. There were stones of different shapes and different colors.

"Map out the shape of a man and arrange those stones according to how your Tutu showed you," Kumu directed. "Each of those stones represents an organ, lumps, ridges, or joint."

Keola arranged the stones in the order that he had been taught. He was so familiar with the anatomy of a man that he had no trouble laying them all out. The colors were almost the same as the stones that Tutu used at home.

He checked his work after he was done laying out the stones that he knew. But there were still more stones that had not been used. "I have extra stones," he admitted.

"The stones that you have laid out are excellent. You already possess an excellent knowledge of the physical form of man," Kumu explained. "Each of the stones that you have left over should be arranged within the head of the figure you have created. Those stones represent an aspect of the psyche of man. In order to be an excellent healer, you must be able to identify the causes for sickness in addition to identifying the sickness. If you do not identify the causes for the sickness, then your patient will never heal, because those behaviors that made them sick in the first place would have been undiagnosed and left to rot in the victim's body. The illness will return and it will continue to return until the patient dies."

Keola pondered what he was being taught. "I understand about the three types of sickness: the punishment from family gods, the obvious body injury, and problems within the family that lead to sickness." Keola continued, "But I do not understand about illness caused by behavior."

"Ahi knew that he was sick. He knew that he was sick for a long time. He could barely walk in here. But when we checked him, what did you notice?" Kumu asked Keola.

"He did not have any obvious injury. He was not bleeding. He did not have any broken bones, and he did not have any external cuts."

"Correct." Kumu prodded, "What else?"

"When we asked him about any problems in his relationships with his gods or with his family, he said that there weren't any."

"Correct." Kumu asked again, "What else?"

Keola replayed the visit in his head. He went over every second and was still stumped. He did not know what Kumu was trying to get at and he felt like he had let himself and his Tutu down.

As if sensing what Keola was thinking, Kumu looked at him and said, "It is very important that for the time you are with me that you let yourself make mistakes, because that is the only way that you are really going to learn. If you knew everything, you would not be here. Now think. What was it about Ahi that we should have paid attention to?"

Again, Keola replayed everything from the moment that Ahi arrived until the time that he went to bed. He recalled the diagnosis session and went over, in detail, the questions that were asked. He recalled leading Ahi to the guest bedroom and helping him to lie down. Then he remembered putting his clothes away. "He had a suitcase filled with clothes!" Keola exclaimed. "Why did he have a suitcase with clothes?"

"Exactly. He knew he was going to die here. He did not know how long it was going to take him to die so he brought a suitcase filled with clothes," Kumu replied. "But he knew he was going to die. Everyone knows when there is something wrong with their body. Sometimes the symptoms are sharp and cause a lot of pain, or sometimes the symptoms are a dull type of pain that sneaks up on them. But it does not matter. People can tell when they are sick."

Keola took it all in and was glad that he was learning so much. He had much to share with Pua. He couldn't wait to tell her his new teachings.

CHAPTER 28

"When we call the family tomorrow, there will be much healing to be done." Kumu added, "We still do not know why he chose to die here instead of with his family. They will have questions, hurt, and anxiety about his illness."

"Perhaps he came here so that his family could be healed," Keola suggested.

"Yes. That is a good theory. But if the family does not acknowledge that there was a problem then there is nothing further that we can do. He could have chosen to spend the final hours with his family but he did not choose to do that," Kumu replied. "Let's go to bed. There is much to do tomorrow."

Keola walked over to the recliner and picked up Kumu. He carried him to the bathroom so that he could brush Kumu's teeth.

Keola placed him in the bed and covered him with a light sheet.

Then he walked outside to look at the moon. When he got outside, he looked into the clear sky with the bright stars. Above the tops of the large breadfruit trees, Keola could see the moon, Mohalu.

Tutu's Story

The Wondrous Child from Kalaupapa

TUTU KNEW THAT PUA AND TIKI must have had a fight. She had not seen Tiki for a few days and she heard crying at night. She decided not to interfere. Instead, she told Pua, "Tiki must be working really hard. I have not seen him in a few days."

Pua looked at her grandmother. She knew that she was fishing for an answer to find out what was going on with the both of them, but Pua could not talk about it. Besides, if Tutu really knew what happened, that would be the end of Tiki in their lives. Pua did not know what she wanted to do and she was also not ready to handle the questions that she knew would follow.

She also did not want to ruin the relationship that Tiki had with Mr. and Mrs. Helekunihi. Pua did not want to expose everything or ruin his life because of one moment of anger. She absentmindedly touched her forehead. She could still feel a little bump where the pail had cut into her head. She was so distracted by it that she did not hear Tutu call her.

"Pua! Where is your head? I have called you three times. You are daydreaming," Tutu chided. "I want to tell you about my cousin Laka, the wondrous child from Kalaupapa."

TUTU BEGAN:

Sometimes man is his own worst enemy. There have been events in history that are so terrible that we don't want to face them. There are things so terrible that if we were to allow ourselves to understand the full weight of what we had just done, it would not be possible to live.

We should learn from our histories that if we are ever to work toward peace that we must learn to recognize when we are making mistakes that harm other people.

It is important for a healer to be in touch with the sense of guilt and trauma that reside within us all. It is even more important that healers learn how to see their own faults.

There have been so many events in our history that stand out as criminal. The massacre of the First Peoples on the continent of North America was terrible. The genocide of the Jewish families in Germany was terrible. Even here in Hawaii, we ourselves have the ugly history of leprosy and Kalaupapa on Molokai.

Everyone says that leprosy came from China—they called it Chinese sickness. I am not sure about this. But I am sure that so many families suffered because of this illness.

When we were young, my father, grandfather, and brother and I caught the steamship from Oahu to go to Molokai. On Molokai, we got on horses and went to the house of an aunt and uncle. We ate and rested.

The next morning we got up really early, had breakfast, and then we made our way down the mountain to Kalaupapa. It was such a long trek. The entire mountain was covered in greenery. From all along the mountain, going down, you could see the ocean. When the sun hit the blue water, it shimmered like the scales of the parrotfish.

There was just a single-lane path going down to the village. It was steep. And it was narrow. I was just a small girl but I remember my grandfather carrying me part of the way when I got sore from riding the horse. I don't remember how long it took us to get down, but I remember that we all traveled together and we didn't say anything the entire way down.

I didn't know anything about Kalaupapa except for what I had heard from the other kids. Only the adults talked about it, but whenever you got near them, they would tell you to go away, or they would change the subject.

What I did know was that leprosy was a death sentence. And sometimes, entire families who lived in the same house would get it except one person. There was no predicting who would catch it. It disfigured your body. Sometimes you would lose your fingers and toes. Sometimes you would have enlarged nerves, but there was always severe pain.

When leprosy became a big problem, they would go to the homes of the people, collect them, and then put them on a boat with some provisions. When the boat got outside of the Kalaupapa harbor, the crew would throw the people off and let them swim ashore. The people that could not swim, drowned. Or the people who were already there stole their provisions. It was a cold and dark time because the people were reduced to living like animals.

When we went to Kalaupapa, the people had established a community. It was still hard for the people to live there because they were isolated from the rest of the world, but at least they did not have to live in deplorable conditions.

When we reached the bottom, my grandfather chanted. I still remember this chant because it was the most beautiful chant I have ever heard in my life. I know now that this was because my grandfather was filled with love for the person he was chanting to, his daughter. In addition, sometimes when I am lying in bed late at night, I can hear the voice of my grandfather drifting over my head into the ears of my aunt:

My sweetheart,
this is the Hoaka moon of the morning,
mourning over the verdant cliff of Kalaupapa.
Kalaupapa, of the broad flat land.
Oahu is empty because you have left,
taken flight to the forest like an apapane,
the apapane whose feathers float around the edge of the moon.
True is this love for you my child of Kamalie.
The gentle waters of Kaiaka are for you,
the sweet waters of Kawaihapai are for you,
the fertile waters of Ukoa are for you,
the red waters of Waimea are for you,
the flowing waters of Anahulu are for you,
the twin waters of Waialua are for you.
Love for you, my child.

The love of a father calls out to you.
Grant me your nose.
Let us share a breath.
It is I.

As I listened to the song, I was overcome with a grief so profound that I started to cry. It was the experience of the entire journey. I adored him. He was such a terrific and honorable man. I will never ever forget that day because I promised myself that I would listen to the teachings of my grandfather in earnest.

Your Uncle Hanalei felt the same way, because he was on the other horse with my father and he was crying as well.

One day when you have a child of your own, you will realize how terrible it was for my grandfather to have lost a child this way. She was imprisoned at that place and it was likely that she would never again see the home where she was raised.

My grandfather knew that this was probably going to be the last chance that he would ever have to see his daughter again. He was too old to make these kinds of journeys. At that time, it wasn't like now where we can hop on a plane and be on another island in an hour or so. In those days, making a trip to the neighbor island was a big ordeal. My grandfather had insisted that we all go. He wanted the entire family to be together again. It is funny how when we are faced with such tragedy, such as the imprisonment of a family member, that the only thing that really matters, when all is said and done, is the love of a family.

My aunt came to the fence—there were two fences that divided the visiting family from the family that was imprisoned in that horrible place. I know that people who live there now enjoy the serenity of that lovely place with its good fishing and peaceful life. But back then it was a horrible prison.

I did not remember this aunt. She was my father's sister, but I had never met her before. I did not know how long she had been in Kalaupapa. All I could do was stare at her.

I could see my grandfather in her. She had his straight, black hair and high cheekbones. She was tall and slender like my grandfather and my father. Her back was as straight as the cliffs that we had just descended. Her skin looked as smooth as a silk pillow. There was no way that she could be sick, I thought to myself.

My father and grandfather went to the place in the fence that was directly opposite her. My father let out a wail that was deep and pitiful. We cried an entire ocean of tears that day.

My grandfather came to me. Uncle Hanalei and I were holding hands. Even though this happened over sixty years ago, I still remember it like it was yesterday. Aunty was wearing a blue-and-white gingham dress that covered her entire body. She looked regal but there was also a pain and bitterness about her.

We poked our little fingers through the fence as if we could touch her but it was no use. There was too much distance between the two fences.

My grandfather called the guard that was sitting between the fences and making sure that none of the patients crossed over the line or did anything that they would regret later. If I remember correctly, this was because of the incident a few years earlier when Piilani had written about the travels of her and her husband, Kaluaikoolau, in the mountains in Kauai. Piilani and Kaluaikoolau were afraid because they had defended themselves against some officers when the sheriff had opened fire on them first. An officer was killed and they were forced to flee into the hills. Everyone was tense.

The guard arrived and grandfather gave him two packages. One was for my aunty and the other was for the guard.

The guard smiled and took the two packages. He kept the one that was for him and he gave the other one to my aunt. She reached inside the pocket of her dress and pulled out a letter. She gave the letter to the guard and he, in turn, gave it to us.

My grandfather gave the letter to my father because he never learned to read. He was the most excellent healer that I have known but he did not know how to read or write. Everything was committed to memory. He was a brilliant man.

My father gingerly opened the letter and read it. I still do not know what was written in that letter, but at that time, I could not have known that this letter would change the lives of our family forever. He stopped and then he looked back at the letter. Then he looked at my aunt in what I can only describe as disbelief.

When I turned to look at my aunt, people had gathered around her. It was not often that there were visitors to the settlement and you could tell the people were curious about us.

But the people who gathered around my aunt did not look like her. Many of them were disfigured with large lumps and bumps.

There were even little children. Some were even younger than myself. There was one girl who came. She could not have been more than seven years old. She approached my aunt and my aunt looked at her and picked her up. The poor thing had already lost her fingers on her hands. She was carrying around a doll with ringlets of brown hair and a dress made of gingham. Yes, that girl could have been me.

My aunt carried her with no problem. My aunt was not scared. She was patient and loving. That day has always been monumental to me because I learned a lot about behavior and how we are supposed to behave. Healers are supposed to be different. We are supposed to accept all people. We are supposed to make them feel safe so that we can work with the patient to help them get better. Many of the things that I have taught you and Keola are from the lessons that I learned that day.

I was really glad that my grandmother had not lived to see this. Her death had spared her the agony of this horrible situation. And amid the isolation of this beautiful place where my aunt was imprisoned, my father was weeping, and my grandfather was weeping. I had never been so upset in my entire life. And it was for many years after that incident that I still questioned my father's intent in taking me there. My mother was right in not coming. It would have been too hard on her to see everyone like that because of the softness of her heart.

My grandfather looked up and called to the guard, who came right away. They whispered to each other before the guard went over to my aunt. They spoke and she smiled. She put her fingers between the wires of the fence and looked at us as my father and grandfather picked up my brother and me. We left. I never saw her again.

We had stayed for only an hour. We had traveled by horseback from our little town for a few days in order to get to the harbor in Kou. After that, we took a steamship for what seemed like a long time. We had left early in the morning to make this trip. And the only time that my grandfather and my father could have there was about an hour.

We started up the cliffs to get back to the village. My grandfather started to head to the beach. We were all silent.

I do not know what he was thinking at that moment. And as I think about it now, more than sixty years later, I know that had to be one of the saddest days of his life.

He walked along the beach edge. The wet sea spray made my cheeks wet. And I remember that I was hungry. But we stayed. We sat at the water's edge and stayed.

I don't know what made my grandfather decide to leave. But he stopped gazing into the ocean and told my father it was time to go.

We made it up the cliffs and got to my aunt's house before dark. Uncle Hanalei and I ate and then took a bath before we went to bed. My father and grandfather tended to the horses and then all the adults went outside to talk. From the bedroom, I could see the oil lamps. I could hear the muffled conversation that was going on outside but I was so tired and I went to sleep.

MY FATHER NUDGED ME AWAKE BEFORE the sun came up. He woke up Uncle Hanalei as well and told us to wash up and get ready for breakfast.

We did as we were told but when we sat down to eat, I noticed that my grandfather was not there. "Is Papa not coming to eat?" I asked my father.

"Papa had to leave earlier. We'll see him back in Honolulu," my father told me.

I was kind of sad to leave because I thought we were going to have more time to visit with that side of the family. But my father said we were going and that was final.

We ate. Cleaned up. Said our good-byes and left. And to this day I have a soft spot for Molokai. In spite of the things that happened in Kalaupapa, the island and the people are beautiful.

The steamship ride was an experience. Did I tell you that it was the first time I had ever left Oahu? I had never been on a ship before and to me it was huge.

Uncle Hanalei and I ran all over the ship just to see everything. All the people on board fascinated us. They were all dressed so nicely. All the men wore suits and all the women wore beautiful dresses or coats. Some of them had the loveliest hats that I had ever seen.

After a lot of running around, we joined our father for lunch. He unpacked the meals that our aunt had made for us and we started to eat. I turned to the left and I saw this handsome gentleman peeling some kind of fruit. I didn't know then that it was an orange. Goodness, I had never seen one before. He started to peel it and it looked so delicious. I was just staring at that piece of fruit that he had. I was absolutely fascinated by it.

Anyway, he caught me staring at him and he did the most gracious thing—he offered it to me. "No thank you, sir." My father kindly waved the fruit away. I was so disappointed. But like I said before, my father was the law. Whatever he said, I did.

"I have another one. Please. It would give me great joy to share this orange with your children." He smiled at my father.

"Thank you, sir. That's very kind of you."

The man gave us the orange. My father peeled it for us. He gave me half and he gave Uncle Hanalei the other half. I did not want to eat mine. It was so perfect. It smelled like sunshine.

Uncle Hanalei ate his in a single gulp. But not me. I took a wedge and let it rest on my lips first. I wanted to enjoy this piece of fruit for as long as I possibly could. I didn't even know where something as delicious as this came from. I didn't even care, actually.

When I bit into it, the juice dripped down my chin and I laughed. We don't think of the simple things that make life worth living. At that moment, I was the happiest that I could possibly be. I was on a steamship eating an orange.

My father turned to the gentleman, extended his hand, and introduced himself. "Thank you again. My name is John. These are my twin children, Joseph Hanalei and Mary Lei."

Our father looked at us. "What do you say to this gentleman?"

In unison we responded, "Thank you."

The man laughed and smiled. "They are wonderful. My name is William L. Green. Nice to meet you."

I remember this man as clear as day because he had death clinging to him. When I say he had death clinging to him I mean that he had defilement hanging from him. He had been around dead bodies and he was doing something to them that was upsetting their spirits. If I knew this word at my age then, I would have called him a grave robber. He reeked of death. He was nice to my brother and me but he had done something terrible and I felt sorry for him because I knew that he would pay for that and the price was going to be terrible. I think my dad sensed it too. It was the reason he had tried to refuse the orange.

YOUR UNCLE AND I RAN OUT TO THE SIDE of the boat to watch it pull into the harbor. And even though we had not been away for a long time, I was happy to see my island.

There was a story in the newspapers about a man who came home after a long trip and as the ship pulled into the harbor, he said:

My rock is in Honolulu.
The island is my shining heaven.

And I knew exactly what he meant.

As the ship pulled in, I was sad that the journey was over but I was happy that I was going home. I missed my mother and I missed my grandfather.

We ran back to my father and we put our coats back on and waited for him to collect our things before we boarded the transport boat that would take us to the pier.

It had ended so quickly. I had just had this marvelous adventure to another island aboard a steamship. We rode horses. I met my father's sister. It was a whirlwind of a trip.

When we got to the dock, our Uncle Ala met us. He helped us load our bags onto the carriage that he had waiting and we got on and went to his house.

"Is Papa at your house, Uncle?" I asked.

"Yes. He is waiting for you." Uncle Ala smiled.

When we got to the house, I heard a baby crying. I thought that Uncle Ala's wife, Yuko, had another child. And I got very excited. Even when I was a young child, I adored children.

I hopped off the carriage and ran into the house. Papa was there with Aunty Yuko. And Aunty Yuko was carrying a little infant. "Can I carry him, please, Aunty?" I squealed.

My aunt looked at my grandfather. My grandfather nodded his approval, so she handed me the baby.

As soon as this baby was in my arms, I knew that I would love him forever. There was such a warm light coming from him. He was a tender, good-hearted baby. In fact, everyone who touched him fell in love with him.

I did not know it at the time, but this baby would change my life forever. He was not Aunty Yuko's baby. He belonged to the aunt that I had just met from Kalaupapa. And he had been born without any arms and legs.

I WOULD BE LYING TO YOU if I told you that I knew the details of how my grandfather got the infant. I do not. During my grandfather's lifetime, I never heard him speak of it. Not even once. My father later said that the reason that he did not talk about it was to protect the people who helped him to get my cousin. There was much fear at that time about the things that went on there.

I imagine that the security guard who treated my grandfather and my aunt with so much respect on that day played a part in all of this. I believe that my aunt made the choice to give Laka to my grandfather under great sacrifice. She knew she would never see her son ever again.

I can also see my grandfather, already in his fifties, making another trek in the darkness down the cliffs of Molokai. I imagine a secret meeting and many, many tears between my aunt and my grandfather.

But he took all that with him to his grave. My grandfather did not break promises. Whoever helped him that night probably asked my grandfather never to reveal his or her identity. My grandfather never did.

Our entire family adored this beautiful child. He was kindhearted and never made much fuss. And we, in return, loved him and treated him as our favorite.

As a child, he was also the most brilliant among us. He had the ability to understand complex concepts and memorize the details for the most strenuous of treatments. He was so smart that no one ever doubted that he would become a healer like us.

Your Uncle Hanalei and I always had to catch up to him. Laka was your Uncle Hanalei's best friend and his archenemy. Sometimes they were very competitive with each other. It drove my grandmother and my grandfather to distraction. But there were always the three of us. We were inseparable.

When it was time for school, my father would carry Laka to the schoolhouse every day. In the afternoon, he would meet us after school and pick us up. He would carry Laka all the way home. The teachers adored Laka because he was so personable and brilliant. It was also a small school and two of father's cousins were the teachers there. We just took everything for granted that life was always like that. It was the only life that we knew.

When Laka was too big for my father to carry, he built a wagon for him. It had four wheels and we just pushed Laka everywhere that we went.

When we studied, Uncle Hanalei and I would take turns helping to turn the pages of the book or to write out his homework. We did this every day until we all graduated from high school.

Our lives were so rich as young children. Even though we had no money, we were privileged children. And I realize now that I tried to make the same kind of experience for you and Keola. I wanted you and your cousin to live together and to train together.

My cousin prefers to live along the Waianae coast. The weather is drier and hotter and it helps some of the ailments that he has. He has dedicated his life to healing and I have not seen him since Uncle Hanalei's funeral. It is okay, though, because he has been doing good, good things.

I want you to think about that now. I want you to think about the life that you have. It is very important and it is very worthwhile. You will be a great healer and so will Keola. But for now, you must let him do what he has to and you must do what you have to. I know that you are hurting and wanting to see him. But it is just temporary. Keola needs to learn the things that he has to learn. And you can support him by letting him go for a little while. He will come back, I promise.

I told you this story about Laka because I wanted to let you know that the important thing is that you are loved. Don't push other people away because you are saddened that Keola is gone. Find joy and comfort in the people that are around you.

"I love you." Tutu smiled.

"I love you too, Tutu." Pua rose to give her grandmother a hug.

"Sweet girl." Tutu hugged her granddaughter. "I am feeling hungry for some mullet. I am going to the fishpond." Tutu got up from her chair to get ready.

Tutu went into the room. She shut the door behind her, opened her closet door, and pulled out the small box that occupied a small space in the very back. She placed it next to her as she sat on the bed. Slowly she opened the box and sifted through it until she found an old, faded photo.

The photo was torn and yellowed with age but she could still see the tall, magnificent woman in the dark suit. It was a picture of her aunt. She was standing in front of a tall, mature mango tree.

Tutu took out the picture and hugged it. Slowly, tears started to roll down her cheeks. She looked at the picture again. "My grand-daughter thinks that the story that I told her is about her and Keola. It is not."

Tutu caressed the photo and spoke to it. "I want my granddaughter to learn from you and your struggles. It is my hope that she sees that life is what we make it." Tutu placed the photo in the box before securing the lid and placing this keepsake with the other fragile contents back in the closet. "Even if we know what is the cost." Tutu looked up. "Even if we know the cost."

The Last Word

TIKI HAD NEVER FELT MORE MISERABLE; nothing made him happy. Even at night when he thought he would have the refuge of his dreams, there was only pain waiting for him.

He only saw the darkness of his life. He saw only death. He imagined himself alone amid the pandanus groves of Puna and the fires of Pelehonuamea were approaching.

At first, he thought that his separation from Pua was just temporary. He waited hourly for her call. He sneaked by her house hoping to see her caring for her plants or feeding the chickens. But she had caught him once and it had made her so angry that she threatened to call the police if he ever came near her again. He feared that she would never let him see her again so he promised to leave her alone.

But still he waited.

He had waited for four months already and she had not called once. The pain that he went through daily was unbearable. Tiki had even tried to contact his father because he wanted to leave. There was no life here without her.

Tiki had stopped going to work. The only reason he went to work was to make a life for himself and for Pua. Now that there was no chance of that, he stopped going to work altogether.

Mr. and Mrs. Helekunihi tried to help Tiki. They tried to talk to him. They tried to comfort him. They tried to take him to see a doctor. But in the end, he was sinking lower and lower into depression. They loved Tiki like a son. They did not want anything to happen to him, but were helpless. The only thing that they could do was to go and talk to Pua. All he thought of was Pua. But they could not bring themselves to do it.

It was odd that Tiki's love for her had not abated after all these months. Usually, young love has a way of petering out. This was different. His feelings for her did not go away. And Mr. and Mrs. Helekunihi were afraid. They slowly came to the realization that being so near to Pua was not healthy. They started to find out how they could contact Tiki's father so that he could go and live with him. Perhaps he would find a new life there and forget about Pua. This is what they hoped for.

Again, they called the number that Tiki's father had given Kale but the number was disconnected. Then Kale went into the main office to see if his coworker had left any information as to where he was: there was nothing. Then Kale and Lovey Helekunihi drove to Honolulu to look for some clues as to where Tiki's father could have gone to in Maui. They went to the last place where he had lived. They asked the new occupants of the house if he had a forwarding address for the mail: there was none.

After they had exhausted all the possibilities they could think of—including asking some relatives who lived on Maui to go and look for Tiki's father—Kale and Lovey decided that the best thing they could do would be to help him find a place on his own in Honolulu. They would support Tiki financially until he could find work.

Kale and Lovey discussed this idea with Tiki. Although Tiki did not want to leave and did not want to be a financial burden to these two people whom he loved so much, he knew that he needed to put some distance between himself and Pua.

They found a nice studio apartment in Chinatown above a noodle factory. It was tiny, but there was a full kitchen. The owner was Kale's longtime friend from school. The rent was something that they could afford and the landlord had offered Tiki breakfast and lunch if he would sweep the sidewalks and the stairs that led to the apartment. Besides, it was only for a short time because Tiki was going to start looking for work. He had even spoken of going back to school. He was already in better spirits.

Lovey worked herself into a state as she started going through her kitchen to pack knives, utensils, plates, pots, and bowls for Tiki's new apartment. She went through her linen cabinet for towels, dishcloths, and washcloths. She was happy that Tiki was looking forward to the move. But most of all she was happy because she felt like she was needed. She loved him so much. She knew that he would always be in their lives. On the weekends, Kale had promised her that they were going to go and see Tiki. They could stroll through Chinatown together and have lunch. She was looking forward to this new adjustment.

Lovey packed all the items into boxes and set them aside for Tiki to carry to the car. She also gave him some blankets, sheets, pillowcases, and some other things from the hall closet. She went into Tiki's room to get an empty box and saw that there was still some room in another box that Tiki had left on the bed. She carried it into the hall and set it next to the closet so she could look through the things and decide what to give him. After she had chosen some simple white sheets, she opened the box to put the linens inside.

When she opened the box, she thought she had grabbed the wrong box because there were papers and envelopes that had been casually thrown into the box. She picked one up to see if it was important.

Dear Son,

Forgive this letter. Perhaps I have no right to contact you. It will be my last offense, I promise. It has been so long since I have seen you. You are a grown man already.

I could say that I have been happier since you left our tiny island but I am not. I could say that I made the right choice but I am no surer of that now than I was on the day that I sent you away.

Your grandmother died a few months ago and I almost sent for you even though she had asked me never to call you back here. We buried her in the cemetery at Paopao. The most important people of our island and those of the island across the channel attended her funeral. Even the most celebrated healers came to honor her. Some of the very ones who hated and were jealous of her for her skill! But why do I go on so? Are you interested in this? Perhaps your heart is still as bitter as the noni fruit.

Before she died she asked my brother to take her once more to Farehape. They went to Papenoo and bathed in the ocean before the long drive to the place where she was born—near the pond of Maroto. He carried her down the hill so she could bathe one last time in Pele's bath.

When they came back up, my brother said that she touched the centipede stone. As your grandmother touched the centipede stone, she saw something that she did not expect—a child. A child was connected to our family stone. The child was half centipede and half shark—oh, what a strong bloodline it has and a strong healer he will be. Yes, it is a boy. He whirled around your grandmother's arm and stung her many times but this medicine could not save her. And it was your child—she was sure of it. You will be a father! Your child carries the memories of healing from my mother and me. He will be the next in our line to use poison to heal. He will be the first there to have the centipede as his god. But this is only if he lives.

But you could see all of this, couldn't you, my love? Just like how you can see that I am dying from the sickness.

You know your fortune as well. You know what your destiny is. I write you to remind you of that. Although I know you carry the thought of it with you every day. How can you forget the words of the Taua from so long ago: You will kill your wife and child.

Do not go against the gods, my son.

Consider it a request from a foolish woman. Consider it a request from a mother who has known what it is like to lose a child.

Perhaps it is the weak character of this woman, your mother, to try and reach out to you now even though I know by the time you get this I will be gone to the land of Taaroa. I am at the end of this letter, but still, I do not know if I have the courage to send it.

Our paths determine our life, not the destination. I am tired. I know that I will have much to answer for when we meet in the land of no return. I have done so many things—what is the use of apologizing? It is too late, I know.

The house and the land are yours should you ever decide to come back home. The house is boarded up and the contents have been left for you. Consider it an apology. Although I know you will never come back. I do not blame you.

I can only say please learn from my mistakes and remember that you are loved.

Aroha nui,

Mama.

LOVEY STARTED TO SHAKE. When she heard the front door open she quickly put the letter back into the box and scurried to put the box back in Tiki's room. As she returned the box to its original place on the bed, she wondered if she had made the right decision. But in the end, she realized that the choice was Tiki's. If Tiki wanted to share the letter, he would.

She walked over to the linen closet and pulled out the warmest blankets she could find. She put them into another box along with some pillowcases and some crisp, white sheets that smelled like the cool mountain wind. For a second, she thought she heard the cry of a baby.

The Leaf Lives

KEOLA HAD A HARD TIME SLEEPING. He had only been here a short time and he had already learned many things. He especially loved to learn about the nature of man and how that translated into healing.

Up until he started training with Kumu, he thought himself a very able healer. But the longer he trained with Kumu, the more he started to realize that knowing the names of plants and how they interacted with the human body was only a small part of being a healer.

The more that Keola studied with Kumu, the more Keola could appreciate his teacher's skill and talent. Kumu had no arms and no legs. This meant that he could not use gestures to communicate. His ability to communicate and to communicate effectively came from his inability to rely on his hands or feet. He could not describe height, or width, or length by simply making the shape with his hands and fingers.

Kumu could not point in a direction. He could not use his fingers to specify numbers like one, or five. These were not things that he could do. Instead, he developed the way that he spoke and the tone of his voice. Just by using simple inflection, he could communicate distance. Just by using simple inflection, he could communicate height, width, and length.

Keola learned these things from Kumu.

Kumu also had a way with people. He was not only kind and considerate but he was also comforting and firm. People trusted Kumu.

Keola noticed that whenever two people spoke to each other, the first thing they did was to establish a physical space between them.

This was based on the type of conversation that they were having and their prior relationship with each other. People did this instinctively. If they were having an intimate moment, then they would come closer together in order to speak with each other. If they were casual acquaintances then the space between them would be greater. This was important because a power dynamic was established. This was important because trust and confidence were also established in this manner.

Kumu did not have this ability because he could not move. The amazing thing is that Kumu raised or lowered the volume of his voice in order to establish this space. If Kumu was giving detailed instructions on the use of medicine, Keola noticed that Kumu would lower his voice until it was almost a whisper: patients instinctively moved closer in order to hear him. Kumu could then give the instructions in a tone that let the patient know that he could be trusted. Or, once they were closer to him, he smelled their breath. A lot of times, illnesses could be diagnosed by the odor of someone's breath.

The voice was a powerful tool of the healer. The tone of the voice and the words that they used changed the space between the patient and the healer, just as it does between a parent and a child. If a parent yells at a child, then the child feels bad and the air around them is negative. If a parent says, "I love you," or praises the child, then the air between them is positive. Keola noticed that Kumu was a master of his voice. He started to employ the same techniques when he spoke to patients, and although he was not as effective as Kumu, he started to learn how to communicate with patients.

Keola was very upset about Ahi. Death was a very real possibility for every patient that he saw. He did not like to think about death but he understood it. It was the worst possible feeling to lose someone that you were trying to help. But he had learned a vital lesson today. He had learned that sometimes people just needed to be comforted in their final moments. Keola would have tried to do more treatments. He would have tried to prolong a life that had already accepted that it was time to leave.

As Keola looked up from his bed to the bedroom window, he could see that the first rays of the sun were already starting to throw their light onto the mountains.

He smiled when he remembered Uncle Hanalei's teaching about the sun.

"Because the Earth is round, the first thing that the light hits is the tallest thing, like the mountain. If you want to estimate how long the sun will take to rise out of the ocean, just turn around and look at the mountains. They will get the sun before you do if you are standing on the shore," Uncle Hanalei said.

Keola really missed Uncle. He was cut from the old cloth of Hawaiian men. He was strict but loving. He was a fisherman and a farmer. He could fix anything. The family respected and admired Uncle Hanalei. He always had time for his family. He had the best stories. And Keola always felt safe whenever he was around. But most of all, Uncle Hanalei had taught him the prayers that he needed to be a healer.

Uncle Hanalei had taught him the prayers to feed his family gods, the prayers to gather plants for medicine, the prayers to heal, the prayers to close the healing, and the prayers to inspire life.

Suddenly, Keola heard the voice of Kumu: "Keola, come get me now."

Keola jumped out of bed and ran into the next bedroom where Kumu was lying.

"We have visitors. Pick me up and put me in the chair in the living room," Kumu said. Keola obliged and put Kumu in the huge chair in the living room.

"Open the door, Keola," Kumu directed Keola. When Keola opened the door, he saw a group of about ten men and women outside the house. A woman's voice from the crowd chanted:

It points this way, then that way.
Kuhi is the omen.
The ones who march are female.
Alaneo is the one that dots the sky.
Apu is the woman.
Halo is the one that spies.
An octopus is for mourning,
an octopus is for celebrating.
Hikikii is female.
Hiku is rounded.
The expanse is Hoolaholaho.

Hoolono is male.
Huliamahi is male.
The ruddy-tinted dog is male,
the reddish dog is male,
the dark dog is male.
Kaapeha is the mass.
Kahaea brings rain.
Kakaula blesses the traveler.
Kalawa clings to the sky.
Kamalii are the children.
Kaniomoe is the battle of chiefs.
Kawauaialii has blacked out the sky for two days.
Kiei looks for a god.
Kiikau drifts in colors.
Koiula beckons repose.
The black clouds of Kane.
Luakalai wears the mantle of seven colors.
For the owl is Mele.
The bird's beak is closed.
Mauna is female.
The five fingers are Nioku.
Ohumu are the plotters.
Onohi is the iridescent pearl.
Opualani is the gathering.
Paemahu stand facing each other.
A sign for the chief is Poloula, a male.
Polokea is female.
The pigs sit on the mountains,
along the horizon
many march in unison.
Uli is female.
Ulu is female.
From Ewa I have wandered this way.
On this path is our quest,
you and I.
Where is my esteemed garland?

My beloved it is I.
A request from a voice.

At the last word, the woman's voice cracked and she began to weep. She was overcome with emotion.

Kumu chanted back:

By the Holo current he came,
by the Moe current he departed.
Waialua is the tranquil waters.
Puu Kanaka the land.
Enter this house of comfort
and together we will weep.
Yes.

Kumu and Keola welcomed the family of Ahi into the house. They went into the bedroom where the body lay and started to weep. Keola looked at all the family members who had arrived. Nothing seemed out of the ordinary. The family was getting along as a family.

From the chant that he had just heard, Keola knew the clouds told them where they would find Ahi. The cloud called Kuhi was the cloud that directed them here. In fact, she had mentioned many cloud forms. Some of them were good omens, and some of them were negative omens.

The woman who had chanted approached Keola. "Thank you very much for caring for my brother." She smiled openly. "He was sick for a long time. Then yesterday morning when we woke up, we noticed that he was gone. We thought that he had gone to look at the ocean. But when he did not come home by the afternoon, we knew that something was wrong."

Keola smiled back at her and took her hand. "He passed quietly and with no pain."

The woman squeezed Keola's hand. "I am glad. The signs in the clouds along the way told us that it was not going to be good news. And when we heard the reply to our chant, we knew that our hunch was correct. Ahi arrived and was alive, but when he left, he went by way of the current called Slumber. His spirit, the two waters that make us, had departed. But I am glad that he went without any pain." She paused.

"We will be heading back now. Please take this small token of our appreciation." She handed Keola a jar of eleele seaweed.

Keola took the jar. Eleele was his favorite seaweed. He loved it in beef stew. He put the jar down, looked out the window, and saw a huge pig cloud sitting on the mountain. It was going to rain.

Lei

IT WAS NOT EVEN LIGHT OUT YET, but Pua had already been up for a couple of hours. She decided that she was going to tell Tutu today about her pregnancy.

She waited until the light in Tutu's room was on and she could hear Tutu rustling about. Even though the door was open, Pua knocked lightly on the door frame.

"Pua! Good morning, sweetheart." Tutu gestured with her arms open.

Pua walked into her grandmother's arms and hugged her tightly. "Tutu, I am pregnant."

"That is terrific, dear! We need more Hawaiian children in this world." Tutu put her palm on the back of Pua's head and pulled her even closer to her. "Tiki must be so happy!"

"Tiki does not know. We had a fight and I have not seen him in a while." Pua pulled away from Tutu and sat on Tutu's bed. "I don't think that I want to see him again."

"Pua, you can do whatever you decide to do. You are an adult." Tutu sat next to her on the bed. "But you must tell Tiki. He has a right to know if he has a child."

"I am going to tell him. But I do not think that we are going to get back together." Pua began to cry.

Tutu hugged Pua. "Everything will be all right. You can tell him when you are ready to tell him." Tutu smiled. "I cannot wait to hear the voice of a little child in this house. I have missed it so."

Pua was reassured by Tutu's support. She was not afraid of the future and for the first time since she had suspected that she was pregnant, she smiled.

Their reverie was interrupted by a voice coming from the front of the yard.

"Hui! Hui! Anyone home?" a woman's voice called out.

Pua went to the front and peeked through the screen door.

"Hi, Mrs. Helekunihi! Please, come inside." Pua lifted the latch and opened the door. "It's nice to see you. How have you been?"

"Fine. I have been fine," Mrs. Helekunihi answered. "I have some fish for your Tutu from Tiki. He went fishing this morning before going back to town and he asked me to give this to your grandmother. He was here for the weekend." She stepped into the house. "Oh, and my flowers were blooming this morning so I made you this lei." She stepped toward Pua to put the lei on her.

"Oh, Lovey! What a beautiful lei!" Tutu stepped between Pua and Lovey and grabbed the lei. "I was just deciding on whether or not I wanted to wear my pandanus hat and you show up with this beautiful lei."

"Tutu, your hat would look so pretty with this as a hatband," Pua exclaimed.

"I think you are right. You don't mind if I use it, would you?" Tutu asked Pua.

Pua replied, "No. Please make use of it. All I am doing today is cleaning the house."

"Well, I think I will use it then when I go to visit Kawika and Haunani." Tutu beamed. "Thank you so much, Lovey. What a terrific surprise and a very friendly gift." Tutu turned to Pua. "Can you please get Lovey some coffee?"

"Yes." Pua headed into the kitchen.

"Actually, Pua." Tutu caught her arm. "I am really craving some tinfish for breakfast: I am famished. Would you mind going to the store to get some?"

"Yes."

"Let me get you some money, dear."

"No need, Tutu. I have some." Pua replied.

"Thank you, dear." Tutu smiled.

Pua exited through the back door. As soon as Tutu could not hear her footsteps on the gravel, she pointed to the kitchen table. "Lovey, let's sit down and have some coffee. You and I can catch up."

Tutu poured coffee into the two mugs. She opened the refrigerator and took out a bottle of cold milk. She placed it on the table and walked over to the drawer to get two spoons. She gave one to Lovey. She opened the tin of sugar and placed it between them. "It is nice to see you, Lovey. How long have you known that Pua was pregnant?"

"I just guessed. I was never sure. You are one of my best friends. I know that you had your reasons for not telling me. But we should talk about this. I am so worried for Pua and Tiki." Lovey took her spoon and swirled the milk and the sugar together with her coffee.

"Where is he now?" Tutu asked. "I heard that he was living in Chinatown."

"Yes. He is living in Chinatown. He couldn't bear it here any more. We could not bear him living here. He was moping around the house for the last four months. He just was walking around with a broken heart. It was so sad and pitiful. We tried to contact his father and grandmother on Maui but we could not find them."

"That is so sad." Tutu added, "Why did they just abandon him? What about his mother?"

"I don't know. Kale and I have been trying to figure that out ever since he came to live with us. We love him like our own. In some ways I don't want to find his father. It was just that he was so sad after the two kids stopped seeing each other." Lovey's voice started to crack. "We thought that maybe it was a good time for him to go back to school and get a place on his own so that he could move on."

"You and Kale did the right thing," Tutu reassured Lovey.

"I think his mother is dead," Lovey said suddenly. "I found a letter from her among Tiki's things. She was from Tahiti. Her letter to him says that she is sick and by the time that he gets the letter she will probably be dead. But in that letter, she talked about her mother. Tiki's grandmother was a healer too, just like you," Lovey continued, excited to get all the details out. "But the letter says that the grandmother went on a short trip to where she was from and she had a vision that Tiki was going to have a child. That's why I wanted to come and see for myself."

"That's why you brought the lei?" Tutu asked.

"Yes. I am so sorry for being so deceitful. But I knew that if she was pregnant she would not be able to wear the lei." Lovey gazed over Tutu's shoulder as if she were trying to summon the strength to say what came out of her mouth next. "Does Pua want the baby? Kale and I have discussed this and we would love to take care of the child if she feels burdened."

"I don't know. She only told me today that she was pregnant. I don't know what her plans are. The only thing that I want is to support her." Tutu smiled. "Just the same as you, Lovey. I am sure that she will figure something out."

"I do not know. Tiki hasn't said anything to me or to Kale." Lovey blew on her coffee before taking a sip.

"I do not know when Pua is going to tell him. Did they ever tell you why they stopped seeing each other?" Tutu asked Lovey.

"No idea. But he was devastated. He almost lost his job because he could not get out of bed. Kale and I asked him if he wanted to talk about it. He never did," Lovey answered.

"Pua, too," Tutu agreed. "She never said anything until fifteen minutes ago." Tutu sighed. "She doesn't want to be a burden."

"Is Keola not here?" Lovey asked. "Maybe she can talk to him."

"No. He is in Waianae getting further training from a cousin of mine." Tutu grinned.

"How long will he be gone?" Lovey asked.

"For as long as it takes." Tutu poured another cup of coffee. "How about some toast and some bacon, Lovey?" Tutu got up and started to prepare some breakfast for the both of them.

"That would be fine, thank you." Lovey held the hot liquid to her lips and inhaled the rich dark smell. If everything could only be as easy as this, she thought to herself.

Tutu and Lovey ate breakfast. It was a simple meal of toast, home-made passion fruit jelly, crispy bacon, and coffee.

The two women chatted about life and the simple things that occupied their day. When Pua came home with two cans of sardines, they each ate a portion of the salty fish.

"Thank you so much for a lovely breakfast. Why don't you come over this evening? I just made some salt meat. We'll have that with some cabbage and poi. I won't take no for an answer." Lovey smiled.

Tutu kissed Lovey goodbye and walked her to the door. Pua packed a bag of cherry tomatoes that she had just picked from the garden. "Thank you so much for the lei. It is really beautiful." Pua kissed Lovey on the cheek.

"Oh, thank you for breakfast and these beautiful tomatoes." Lovey walked out the front door. "I will see you tonight. Bye."

"Aloha."

LOVEY STARTED TO WALK THE SHORT DISTANCE to her home. Her thoughts were of Tiki and his unborn baby.

As a young wife, she had dreamed of becoming a mother, and sometimes the yearning to become a mother had threatened to suffocate her.

Lovey had tried every remedy known to Hawaiian and foreign doctors. Her mother had told her to eat taro leaves. Her cousin had told her to eat the roe of sea urchins. Another told her to eat the eggs of chickens when the moon was in the phase of Hua. There was meaning in the words they told her. All of these things associated with eggs would help her to have a child. Nothing worked.

When she went to the foreign doctors, all they managed to do was to make her depressed. They stuck needles in her. They drew vials and vials of blood. She allowed them to prod and poke her and it almost caused her to kill herself. The doctors were so invasive.

Twice she had been promised a child. Her cousin had once decided to give Lovey her infant, a girl. Her cousin was married to a man from the continent and he did not understand Hawaiian adoption. He had forbidden the adoption even though they already had seven children. Lovey was devastated.

One year after that, Kale's sister gave birth to a child that had Down syndrome. His sister was distraught and did not know what to do. Lovey and Kale offered to take the child and raise it as their own. A child is a gift, Lovey thought. She had enough love in her heart for a million children, she thought. The child died a few days after it was born.

Lovey thought no more of having children. Her heart could not bear any more disappointment. She simply convinced herself that she never wanted to have children.

Lovey became the best wife. She became the perfect wife, friend, sister, sister-in-law, cousin, neighbor, devoted Catholic, and woman.

In her heart she would have given it all up in order to become a mother. Her heart closed itself off to the idea of ever having children of her own, or of ever having children to raise as her own.

When Kale asked if he could bring Tiki home for a few weeks, Lovey had no idea how much joy he would give her. He rekindled all of her motherly feelings that she thought she had lost a long time ago.

And even though she wanted him to always be safe and happy, she was secretly relieved that Tiki's father could not be found. She was even a little happy that there was no longer a threat of him ever being taken away by his natural mother.

Lovey was proud of herself for working through her issues with Tiki. At first, she thought it very strange that a parent would want to abandon his child. The incident with Mr. Keahi, her neighbor, had riled her but she did not blame Tiki. She would never understand why Mr. Keahi said those hateful things about Tiki. Tiki was innocent. He was a good boy. He fished for them. He was thoughtful and considerate.

Even though Tiki was a grown man, she had allowed herself to love him as much as a mother loves her child. She thought of him every day. She called him every day to make sure that he had eaten. She made sure he came home on the weekends so that she could wash his laundry. Before he left on Sundays to go back to his place, she packed him food that she had prepared. Even though he told her not to, she would always slip some money into the little care packages that she made for him. Living alone was rough, she explained to him, and she would just feel terrible if he had to do without something because he did not have the money. Lovey and Kale also told Tiki that they would pay for his school and books if he decided to go to college. Tiki protested but it was to no avail. She would do anything to protect him and to support him. Anything.

Lovey walked home at a slow pace. Her thoughts, however, were racing. She decided that as soon as she got home she would call Tiki. His classes ended at 11:30 and he would be at home eating lunch before he went to work.

TIKI BELIEVED THAT HE COULD SEE GHOSTS. In fact, he knew that he could see ghosts. They passed him on the street. They sometimes came into class with him. Sometimes, the bold ones would dare to come into his house. But he did as his grandmother had told him and did not pay them any attention.

"One day you will learn how to communicate with them and get their help," his grandmother had said. "Until then, ignore them. If one of them becomes a nuisance, then yell at it. Call it every dirty name you can think of. Scream at it to go away."

He lived by this advice. Sometimes, he could sense their pain. It was as if they were trying to find their way and he felt sorry for them. But he did not reach out. He did not know what would happen if he tried to communicate with one of them. He knew that there were good spirits and there were bad spirits. For all he knew, it would be his luck to reach out to a bad spirit that would try to harm him or his family. No. He had no need for them now. It was better to leave well enough alone.

Tiki could also feel people that were close to him, except he did not know the potential of this ability. Even before he had received the letter that told him his mother had died, he knew that she had. He had felt her energy vanish. She did not communicate with him. He could not sense words coming from her. He simply felt her presence. And as soon as he felt it, it was extinguished.

Tiki had not learned to control this ability either. He did not even know that it was an ability; he just thought he had developed a strong intuition about the people that he loved.

He did not realize that this was the truth with all the people he knew. Once while he was at work, he sensed that something was not quite right with one of his coworkers. He dismissed it, however, and continued with his work. That afternoon, the same coworker had a heart attack. Tiki had dismissed his earlier intuition, so he did not remember that he knew something was wrong even before it happened.

One day while he was talking with Kale, Kale mentioned to him that he was going to go to work at the construction site and then go to see his sister. Tiki knew as soon as Kale uttered those words that they weren't true. Kale was not going to make it to his sister's after work. Tiki did not know the reason why he knew it was not true; he only knew that it was. The next day, Kale woke up with horrible gout: He could not get up from bed for the next three days.

Tiki simply believed that these were coincidences. It did not even register with him that there was something else happening. His talents had never been recognized or encouraged. He had never had any training to develop these skills to their fullest potential. He learned to doubt them. He learned to think of his talents as random feelings. All Tiki could be was potential.

And so when he started to think about Lovey, he did not know what was going on. The last hour in class had been excruciating. Tiki couldn't explain it but he was restless. He didn't know what was wrong. It was his favorite class. But all through the class all he could do was think about Lovey. It had started in the morning and as the day passed the feelings started to get stronger and stronger.

First, he just brushed it aside and thought that it was a little homesickness. He really loved Lovey and Kale Helekunihi. Sometimes it was almost unbearable to be away from them. Even just sitting under the mango tree and talking story was one of the things in the world that he most liked to do. On weekends, they went to the beach. He loved to catch fish and then roast them on coral rocks placed on the hot fire. He lived for those things and it made going to work and going to school easier to cope with during the week.

Tiki wanted to leave class. His body itched and he felt flush. And the image of Lovey Helekunihi flashed into his mind again. He was getting up to leave when he remembered that it was Lovey and Kale who were paying for his school. They supported him and it was unfair to them if he just got up and left. They gave him so much—more than his stupid father had ever given him. Yet it was so easy just to tell himself that he was uncomfortable and walk out the door. He was being silly, he told himself. He adjusted himself in his seat and sat for the remainder of the class. He would call Lovey when he got home.

As soon as class was over, he went straight home to his tiny apartment in Chinatown.

He walked into Kam Fat Noodle Factory and greeted the owner. "Hi, Mr. Lum!" He bolted up the stairs, threw his books onto the bed, and dialed Lovey.

"Hello."

"Hi!" Tiki beamed.

"Tiki! You have been on my mind all morning." He could hear the smile in her voice. "Have you eaten?"

"I just got home and was about to make lunch but I thought I would call you first to see how you are doing."

"I am fine. Are you coming home this week?" Lovey asked.

"Yes. Is everything okay?"

"Everything is fine. I made a bucket of salt meat and I wanted to make sure you were here so I didn't waste anything." She paused. "I had breakfast with Pua and Tutu this morning."

Tiki's heart dropped. He almost dropped the phone at the mention of Pua's name. "Are they okay?"

"Everyone is fine. A-okay," Lovey answered. "When you come home, don't forget to bring your laundry. I am glad that you are doing well. How are your classes?"

"Fine. I have a test next week Tuesday so I am going to start studying for it when I come home from work today." Tiki looked out the window.

"Okay. I'll let you go. You sound busy. Don't skip any meals and make sure you get enough rest," Lovey said, caringly.

"I will. I promise. See you this week." Tiki got up to place the phone back on the cradle.

"Yes. See you this week. Bye."

"Bye."

"Oh, Tiki?" Lovey whispered.

"Yes?"

"I love you. Come home safely." Lovey hung up the phone.

"I love you too." Tiki put the phone down and walked over to the kitchen to prepare his lunch. He warmed up some spaghetti that Lovey had made and packed for him on the small stove in his studio. It was the best spaghetti he had ever eaten.

WHEN TIKI FINISHED HIS LUNCH, he changed into his work clothes and started down the stairs. Mr. Lum was busy with customers.

Tiki grabbed the broom and started to sweep. The foot traffic and the flour from the noodles created a mess on the stairs and the floors and needed to be cleaned several times a day. Tiki made sure that the floors were spotless before he left for work. Mr. Lum was Kale's friend and he wanted to make sure that he did his best.

When he was finished, he put the broom and the dustpan away. He had so much to do. He had to talk to Pua. He had to finish this program at school so that he could move up at work.

School was the reason that he had not approached Pua. He wanted to show her that he could make a worthy husband and father. It was the reason why he really liked learning how to fish with Kale. He wanted to show Pua that he could always feed her.

Tiki got on the bus and headed toward his job. For the first time in a long time, he felt that he was going somewhere.

Keola Dreams of the Woman with the Shark's Mouth on Her Back

IN THE DREAM, KEOLA AND KUMU arrive at the home of a woman patient. Two smiling women greet Kumu and Keola at the door.

When they enter the modest home, they notice the numerous shellacked turtle shells that hang along the wall. There are over thirty turtle shells of assorted sizes and colors. Most shells are black or brown and have a glimmer of dark yellow marbling.

The two healers move into the room where a girl lies on her bed. Keola sees her and gasps in surprise. He runs to the bedside because the girl is Pua.

He takes her face in his hands and starts to cry. What is Pua doing at this house? Who are these people?

He is frantic. He takes her left hand and looks at her fingers. No. It is not Pua. This young woman has all of her fingers.

The resemblance is uncanny. Keola cannot take his eyes off this young woman.

Keola places Kumu in the chair that has been set near the head of the bed for him. "How long has she been sick?" he asks the two women.

"We do not know. We found her on the beach this morning. She was lying on the sand, unconscious," one of the women responds.

"We do not know who she is or where she came from. We know that she is still alive, but we do not know the nature of her illness. Did she drown?"

Keola puts his ear to her chest and listens. Her breathing is clear. There is no water in her lungs.

Keola opens her eyes with his thumb and pointer finger. Her pupils are not dilated. It appears as if she is just sleeping.

"How long has she been sleeping?" Keola asks the two women.

"She has been like that ever since we found her at sunset along the beach. My husband brought her here and then we sent for you," the elder woman replies.

"But we did not call you because we think she is dying," the younger woman adds. "She does not appear to be harmed in any way. We think she is sleeping."

"Then why did you call us?" Kumu asks.

"She has a shark's mouth on her back."

Kumu instructs, "Keola, turn her over gently."

Keola turns over the girl's body. At the top of her back, right between her shoulder blades, is a huge salivating mouth filled with two rows of shark's teeth. The teeth are sharp. The mouth opens and closes as if it is gasping for air.

Keola becomes frightened. The jolt in the dream world wakes him up.

KEOLA RECALLED THE STORY OF NANAUE, a boy who was born with a shark's mouth on his back. The shark-god Kamohoalii, Nanaue's father, gave specific instructions that the young boy was not to eat any meat. However, the boy's maternal grandfather disobeyed the command and gave the young boy a meal of pork. This caused Nanaue to develop a taste for human flesh. He dragged swimmers into his cave and devoured them while they were still alive. Eventually, residents of the area caught and killed him.

Keola thought about the dream and how it could possibly link to the story of Nanaue. Having a shark's mouth was a coincidence. But he was concerned with the story about Nanaue and how it could be linked to Pua. Maybe Pua was in danger.

Keola stared at the ceiling. His thoughts started to race. He could not go back to sleep. This dream was a bad premonition and it needed to be destroyed so that it would not happen.

Keola got out of bed and walked into the living room. He opened the door that led outside and stepped into the warm night air.

Suddenly, he spit on the ground and started cursing. "You stupid dream," he began. "Go back and bite the person who sent you. That is not going to happen to Pua. I cut you. I remove you. This dream is just a bunch of gibberish."

As soon as he was done sending the dream back to its owner, he sat on the patio chair and tried to delve even deeper into the meaning of the dream. Sometimes, the dream is very clear. Everything in the dream is obvious. Sometimes, that is not the case. The dream is filled with layers of meaning and the meaning is not obvious.

He had the urgent need to see his cousin. He would ask Kumu tomorrow to see if he could go and visit her. He had not seen her or talked to her ever since the training started. The months had gone by too fast.

Pua and Keola

PUA AWOKE IN THE MIDDLE OF THE NIGHT. Her first thought was of her cousin, Keola. Instinctively, she rubbed her huge belly when she thought of her cousin. She wondered if he knew she was pregnant. Even though he was just on the other side of the island, she decided not to contact him.

Intense training from a master healer meant that Keola would need all of his energy and focus. She did not want to be a distraction to him. And as much as she needed him now, she put him before herself and said nothing.

Pua knew that Keola understood this as well. It was the reason that he did not call the house. She also knew that if Keola heard her voice, the deep love that he had for her would rise up in him and he might possibly decide to come home.

Pua did not worry that he hadn't called. In fact, she was glad that he did not call because that meant that he was studying hard and absorbing all the information his new teacher was giving him. She was also glad that he did not call because she felt that if she heard his voice she would fall apart.

She rubbed her belly and knew that the child that she was now carrying would be as loved by her cousin as she was. "If you have someone who loves you more than you love yourself, you will be the luckiest person in the world," she whispered to her unborn child.

She would be forever indebted to her mother and to Keola's mother for letting Tutu take the two cousins and raise them. They had grown up in a loving, stable home. They had grown up with an attentive grandmother who was a master in her field. They had grown up on one of the most beautiful parts of the island.

Keola and Pua knew who their mothers were. They visited them often and both of them were very close to their siblings. She did not understand how some people could say that adoption was a bad thing or why some children felt lost. This was totally different from how they were raised. Their mothers were two unselfish women who allowed their mother to raise their children.

It made Pua think. So far, no one had come forward to ask for her child. Maybe someone would come forward and ask as more people knew about Pua's pregnancy. She was unmarried, and that might lead people to think that she could not handle the stress of a child in the home, but Pua was optimistic. She knew that as soon as she spoke to Keola and they worked out a plan, everything would be all right.

Pua's favorite memory of their youth was their time spent playing in the taro ponds. Most especially, Pua and Keola loved to catch the crayfish that littered the ponds. They would catch one crayfish with a net and then rip off its tail. They would use that tail for bait to catch other crayfish. The crayfish would latch onto the bait and then Keola and Pua would simply lift the crayfish out of the water and place it in the bucket. When their bucket was half filled, they would take the bucket to Tutu, who would clean the tails and fry them in butter. It was the perfect lunch.

On days when they did not want to catch crayfish, they would walk along the paths between the taro ponds. The huge green leaves of taro made a flapping sound when the heavy wind came. When the days were really hot, they would take off their slippers and slip their feet into the cool spring water. Oh, how much fun it was to sink barefoot into the mud!

Amid the thick stalks of taro were crunchy roots of lotus. The owners of the ponds often gave Pua and Keola lotus roots to take home. Tutu boiled the roots with beef in soy sauce, sugar, and matchsticks of ginger.

These memories washed over her repeatedly and made her restless. She rarely thought of these things but they were coming back to her now. She remembered walking past Great-grandpa Hale's house on their way to and from school. He cleaned his yard twice a day. In the morning, he raked the leaves. In the afternoon as Pua and Keola returned home from school, he watered his plants. He always had a treat for them to make their walk more enjoyable. Sometimes he had fruit from the trees in his yard. Other times, he would give each of them a dime so that they could buy a piece of candy or shave ice. He was a terrific and kind man who lived until he was 104 years old.

Pua was wide awake. She also knew that Keola was thinking about her at the very same time—she could feel it. She could also feel that he was going to come and visit her.

EVEN THOUGH THE SUN WAS HOURS from coming over the horizon, Pua got out of bed, washed up, and started to cook. If Keola was coming, she needed to make sure the house was super clean and that everything was prepared. As soon as the sun came up, she would go and ask the owners of the taro patch for taro leaves to make octopus, coconut milk, and taro leaves. For now, she decided to start cleaning out a beef stomach to make tripe stew.

While the tripe was parboiling, she decided to start cleaning the windows. She took out newspapers and a concoction of vinegar and water so that there would be no streaks on the glass windows or on the jalousies. She did each perfectly, until she could see her own, clear reflection.

Pua then grabbed the dust cloth and began to wipe down all the surfaces in the house.

She busied herself doing these things. When Keola came home to visit, the house would be sparkling clean and there would be enough food to feed all of Waialua.

After eating and catching up, Pua knew that Keola would want to go to the beach to see Kaleihepule. Pua knew this was going to be a memorable day.

The Fisherman's Chant

TIKI AWOKE IN A RAGE. For the last seven days, the same nightmare had come to him.

Pua was on the beach at Kaiaka picking seaweed. As she bent over to pluck the salty grass from the reef, she sang this song:

From Waimea to Kapohakuokauai.
From Kamananui to Kealia.
From Kawailoa to Kawaihapai.
From Paalaa to Mokuleia.
From Opaeula to Poamoho.
From Wananapaoa to Kainapuu.
From Punanue to Helemano.
From Puaena to Paalaauka.
From Kaiaka to Kaupakuhale.
From Kawaiakaaiea to Kaala.
The wind is Maeaea.
A net for fish.
Where is the fish?
An eyestripe surgeonfish is the fish,
a yellowfish is the fish,
a bluespine is the fish,
an orangespine is the fish,
an achilles tang is the fish,
What is the bait?

The bait for a big fish?
The big-eyed net for the big fish.
I will throw it back,
for it is not delicious.
It is ended.

He did not know what the song was about, but he awoke enraged because he thought that Pua was taunting him.

The more that he thought about it, the more he was enraged. Perhaps these dreams were telling him that he needed to talk to her. He needed to find out if there was a chance that they would ever get back together.

This dream made him mad. Why was Pua drawing him a net? Why was she talking about these reef fish? What did they have in common?

Tiki knew that this dream was a reflection of what he was going through. It probably had nothing to do with Pua. He knew that it was something that his own consciousness was trying to tell him about his relationship with her.

This thing was making him mad. He knew what he wanted and he did not want anyone, including his own self, to tell him that he was not destined to be with Pua. He did not want to face that—even if it was the truth.

When he looked around the house, he could not find Kale or Lovey. He looked outside for them but they were not there either. The yard was a mess, so he decided to clean the yard.

It was hard being away because Kale and Lovey were getting older and it took them longer to get to certain things. Usually when he came home on the weekend he was busy studying or doing laundry. He did not have time to clean the yard or make house repairs. He loved doing things for them. Because they were gone, he decided to start the chores right away so they would not make a fuss that he was cleaning the yard rather than studying.

He raked the leaves around the house. Once that was completed, he took the hose and started to water the plants around the house. As he looked at the plants around the house, he reflected upon his own childhood and the plants that surrounded his mother's house.

CHAPTER 35

His mother had thousands of plants. She knew each one by name. She knew how each one was used. She knew how each one grew and the care that it needed. It was the reason, Tiki believed, that he was attracted to Pua.

Tiki had noticed that even though these two women lived at different times and lived thousands of miles apart, they shared many similarities.

Both women used the same plants to do the same things. They both used taro stalks for the treatment of insect bites. They were both focused. Most importantly, both had their own ceremonies that related them to their practice.

Once, Tiki had driven Pua to the forest to get some plants for medicine that only grew from a certain area. She was very specific with him: he could not talk to her at all before she went to get the medicine. As soon as she entered the forest, her behavior changed. She was very focused. Her body became rigid and she chanted to the forest and the trees. This communication with her element, that region that allowed her to be a healer, was the foundation of her profession. It was the movement of her body within this region that defined who she was.

Tiki appreciated her commitment to who she was. But sometimes, it intimidated him. Sometimes it made him feel lost because he did not have the same direction. He did not have the same relation with land or a region. He did not have a profession. Because he did not have a profession he did not have a ceremony that connected him to these deeper things.

Healers know when certain flowers are blossoming. Healers know when the weather will prevent them from going into the forest. Healers will pray for a plant to heal the patient. Healers will know what ceremonies are necessary to ask for the power of the plant to come forth and heal the patient. They have to know the chants to ask the healing power to enter into their hands. They have to know the chants to pull the healing energy of the universe into the sick patient. Healers study and become experts in the environment and ceremonies of their area.

If a healer uses seaweed to heal, then the healer has to understand tides, ocean levels, growth cycles, and the healing properties of each plant. Healers know that variations in moisture, altitude, amount of sunlight, and soil composition influence the medicinal potency of plants.

An able healer always knows to test the potency of a plant if it came from another area.

Tiki had a number of opportunities to develop the skills that he had been given from his mother. But for various reasons he had not learned how to heal. He had no regrets. That was not his path.

Tiki recognized Pua's accomplishments, but they belonged to her and not to him.

But Tiki had another path. He envisioned a house and a wife and a son. He worked hard to better himself so when the time came he could provide for his family. And as the months went by, that was the one thought that kept him going day after day. He envisioned birthday celebrations and anniversaries. He dreamed of grandchildren. And he would bring all of these things into existence with his hard work.

He rarely thought of culture and of connection and of the deep pathways that connect people to their land and spirit realms. He did not want to connect with those areas. Worse, he felt that they did not want to connect with him.

After he finished watering the plants, he went to the beach to relax.

The Pathways of Kanaloa

The Lesson of Haloanakalaukapalili

KEOLA PLACED SLIPS OF MORNING GLORY in the car. He also placed fingers of bananas, coconut cordage, octopus, and spiderwebs in various gourds on the back seat. He was coming back with these symbols of knowledge. Kanaloa represented this deep knowledge. The physical shape of these things represented the connections that one makes in learning. A length of cordage between two people or between one person and knowledge was a pathway. And just as the plant body forms of Kane required or stored water, the body forms of Kanaloa extended out. Keola felt really good about everything he was learning from Kumu.

Keola learned how to place an octopus on the navel of a sick patient. The octopus would symbolically pull the sickness out and disperse it through its tentacles. The tentacles, like the rope and spiderwebs, were necessary in healing because even though there were no medicinal values attributed to these body forms of Kanaloa, they were spiritual medicine. These objects communicated to patients that they were about to be healed and that they should resolve to get well.

Healers needed this communication with the people they were healing. They also got this from their environment. Once they understood the environment, they were able to understand the way the world works. Once they understood the way it works, they were able to understand the nature of healing. Once they understood the nature of healing, they were able to understand people. Thus, healing was restoring the balance of the universe.

People are their own universe. As Keola had learned, a man is a house. He is a house of water. He is a house of wind. He is a house of fire. And he is a house of dirt. A body, like a house, is a shelter. It is a house of water because there is blood and spit. It is a house of wind because there is breath and gas. It is a house of fire because our bodies generate heat. It is a house of dirt because after the body is dead, it turns to dirt.

Keola had also learned that in order to be a healer that cures people, he would need to access all the gifts that he had been given. These gifts were not limited to the instruction that he received from Tutu and from Kumu. These gifts came from his blood and the very cells that he was made up of. It came from his great-great grandparents, Kealo and Kawanana. It came from his great-grandfather, Kalau.

Keola and Pua were the next in line. Kumu had told Keola that his training was almost finished. Soon, it would be Pua's turn. Soon, she would have the great opportunity that he had.

The knowledge was profound and he was tapping into his ancestral memories as a healer. Ancestral memories are the talents and information that people have in their DNA. Keola wanted to show his grandmother that he had been a good student by listening and learning. He wanted to show her that he was recalling his blood memory—the information he had inherited from her that was now stored in the fiber of his being. He had also been a good student by connecting with this information.

Kumu encouraged Keola to interpret the meanings of things. During his months of training, he had learned to envision a healthy patient. If a patient complained of a sore back, it could be that the patient had been hurt from work. Or a hurt back could be an indication that the patient was suffering from the stress of a burden of some sort that was represented by a backache. Keola had to talk to the patient in order to find out the cause of the backache because that determined the cure.

Finding the correct cure could heal the patient. Diagnosing the patient incorrectly and prescribing the incorrect medicine could be disastrous.

There was a new dimension to the knowledge that he already possessed. Kumu taught Keola that the path to healing was a far more intricate process than he had ever imagined.

CHAPTER 36

There were so many variables in healing that Keola realized the only truth in healing was that the healer never finished learning. Keola would be a student until the day that he died.

Death, birth, and life were what he had learned with Kumu. The story of Haloanakalaukapalili explained this cycle. When Hawaiians die, their bodies were interred in the land. After a time, their bodies became the earth. The earth became a womb for the plants. Men consumed these plants. When a man died, he was returned to the earth. It was a spectacular cycle. This is how Hawaiians are connected to the earth. If a family had lived in an area for generations, their ancestors made the land where they lived and grew their food. The most heinous act was to go against this edict, to sever this cycle. Removing bones severed this cycle.

Keola made sure that everything was packed well and decided to go into the house to check that everything was also well with Kumu. A cousin was going to be taking care of Kumu while Keola was gone.

As he turned to go and say goodbye, he looked into the sky at the scorching sun of Waianae and decided that once he visited a little with Tutu and Pua that he was going to go to the beach.

Tutu Observes the Clouds

TUTU WOKE WITH A START. She got up, put her house slippers on, and went into the living room to see what was going on.

"Pua, what are you doing up at this hour?" Tutu asked.

"Good morning, Tutu." Pua smiled. "Sorry to wake you. I was trying to get some cleaning finished. Keola is coming home." Pua lifted up the lamp to dust the table.

"What? Keola is coming home?" Tutu moved closer to Pua.

"I think Keola is coming home. I had a dream about him coming home." Pua put the lamp down and wiped its base.

"Well, then let me go into the kitchen and make some breakfast. We have a lot of things to do if he is coming home."

Tutu pulled open the drawer next to the sink and pulled out her favorite knife. She pulled out the chopping board that was next to the drying rack, laid it on the counter, and put her knife on the clean surface.

She could tell Pua was making honeycomb tripe by the smell of the flesh and the ginger that was coming from the pot. She opened the refrigerator and noticed all the things Pua had set aside. "This girl is making enough food for the whole island." Tutu laughed.

Tutu realized how important this visit was to Pua. In fact, it was also important to her. She missed seeing Keola every day. She missed talking to him about life and about medicine and about patients. She also wanted news of her cousin, Laka. She had not seen him since Hanalei's funeral and even though he lived on the other side of the island, he was always in her thoughts. Even though he was now a great, re-nowned healer, he would always be the little one whom she helped to raise.

The love that was coursing through her warmed her body and her face began to glow. She closed the refrigerator after grabbing some eggs and the fried fish from the night before.

Morning light started to break as she prepared everything for their breakfast. She walked over to the rice pot to check if there was still some leftover rice for breakfast. The rice looked wet, so she smelled it and noticed it was sour. She took the pot out of the cooker and walked to the back door. She went outside, scooped the rice in her fingers and flung it out to the chickens that were feeding on grass in the backyard. The brown and white chickens clucked over to the white grains lying on the grass and began to feed.

Tutu looked at sun, the man who lights up the heavens, and started to chant:

A fire is ignited above Hahaiole.
A light will touch the sands of Kaohikaipu,
to then fall on Manana.
It will travel toward the mountains and disperse in Luluku,
like a love spreading aimlessly across the skirt of the Koolau
    mountains.
Affection, indeed!

As she said the last line and tapped on the bottom of the rice con-tainer to get the last grains out to the chickens, she looked and saw Uluhala on the branch of the mango tree.

Uluhala is a name that means life and death, growth and passing. That it was on the mango tree, in Hawaiian, manako—the power to fulfill and bring to fruition was a sign that Tutu could not ignore. Some-thing was going to happen today.

She looked around for other signs. She looked upward into the sky. She saw something that made her heart almost stop beating: there was an ominous cloud hovering above the house.

The thick, huge cloud was hanging on both sides and other clouds accompanied it. Tutu recognized this omen.

She scanned the skies for other omens and above those clouds was a large, elongated cloud that looked like a shark.

Tutu turned the rice pot over to get out the last bits of rice and walked back into the house. She washed the rice pot and made a fresh pot of rice. She took the heavy cast-iron skillet and put a little oil into it. As soon as the oil started to give off some wisps of smoke, she cracked the eggs one by one into the skillet. While the eggs were frying, she scrambled them and then threw the morsels of fried fish into the eggs with ringlets of green onion. When the eggs were done, she put them into a bowl and set the bowl on the table. Fish will be good for Pua's baby, Tutu told herself.

Tutu scooped out some steaming rice and placed it on a plate for Pua. She made a small scoop of rice for herself. As sort of an afterthought, she grabbed another plate and placed three heaping scoops of rice on the plate. She took the plates and placed them on the kitchen table.

She took the pitcher of ice water from the fridge and placed it on the table. She went over to the coffee pot to check on the coffee. It was almost done.

She sat at the table and waited for the coffee. In reality, her heart beat a million times a minute. She had learned that sometimes it is the routine of one's life that saves one from going crazy or sliding into help-lessness. The routine of preparing breakfast was saving her right now. She looked up at the large clock that was hanging on the kitchen wall. It read 7:45 a.m.

Fifteen minutes later, at 8:00 a.m., the familiar clunking noise of the family car could be heard barreling down the lane. For a second, Tutu forgot the signs that she had seen in the clouds and let herself smile. "Keola is here, Pua." Tutu got up from her seat and went to the front door.

"I need to get ready." Pua went into the bathroom to freshen up.

Keola slammed the car into park, opened the door, and bounded into the arms of his grandmother who waited for him on the porch. "Tutu!" Keola exclaimed like a child.

"Aue! Grandson!" Tutu began to tear up. "I am so happy to see you."

"Me, too!" Keola lifted his grandmother's hands up to his lips and kissed her palms. "Me, too."

"Go grab your things and bring them into the house. Pua is in the bathroom. She'll be out in a second."

Keola took everything out of the car. He took his things into his room and put the foodstuffs away in the kitchen.

"Let's eat breakfast." Tutu beckoned.

As Keola headed into the kitchen, he knocked on the bathroom door. "Why are you taking so long?" Keola teased. "Do you have diarrhea?"

"Be quiet. Go sit down. I have something to show you," Pua yelled back.

Keola sat down to a feast of eggs, rice, fish, tripe stew, taro tops, and taro paste. "Hurry, Pua. I am hungry. I don't want to wait all day for you," he teased.

Pua walked into the kitchen. As soon as Keola saw her, he got up from his chair and ran to her. He took her into his arms and squeezed her. "You're huge!" He laughed. "When am I going to be an uncle?"

It was the best possible welcome that Pua could have hoped for although she never expected anything different. She smiled.

The family sat down for breakfast. They spoke about Kumu and Keola's training. They ate and caught up. After they were done eating, they sat at the kitchen table and talked until lunchtime.

At lunchtime, Tutu prepared another meal of taro leaf stew. Keola and Pua discussed Tiki's separation from Pua. They made plans that when the time came for Pua to go to training, Keola would care for the infant.

As the hours passed languidly and the discussion moved from serious to lighthearted back to serious, Tutu reflected on the signs she had seen in the morning. How could it be that a loving conversation in the kitchen could lead to such a grave ending?

After eating, Keola leaned back in his chair and patted his stomach. "I look pregnant, too." They covered the taro paste. They spoke about Pua, Tiki, and the pregnancy.

"We must have eaten enough for ten people." Pua laughed.

"And talked enough for twenty." Keola smiled. "It is a nice day. I am going to the beach for a swim."

Pua got up from her chair and started to clear the table. "I will go too after I clean up."

The family cleared the table and put the leftover food away. While they washed and dried the dishes, Tutu looked at the children with longing. Fate is fate. There is no way around it. People either accept it or they do not. Either way, it is still theirs.

She stared at the both of them and tried to imprint each and every curve of their face and hair on their head. She tried to remember each word they said. If it was her time to go, then her only hope was that she could have seen her first great-grandchild. Hawaiian children are precious and she would have liked to have met this one. If the gods were calling one of her grandchildren, then she hoped that she had given them the best life possible. She had fed both of them to the point where they could not eat anymore. She wanted them to leave her house filled with food and filled with love.

As they prepared themselves for an afternoon on the beach by grabbing some towels and making some pork and bean sandwiches, Tutu took the opportunity to see each one privately.

"Pua, I love you. Remember that. Your baby will grow up to be a fine healer." Tutu hugged her granddaughter and smelled her neck.

Tutu walked outside to the shed where Keola was looking for his diving mask and snorkel. "Keola, I am so happy to have you back for a little while. Thank you for taking care of your cousin and her baby. You have become such a terrific man. I am very proud of you." She pulled him to her. "I love you very much."

Pua and Keola did not think anything of these outbursts of affection. Tutu was a very affectionate person. They just thought that she was being emotional because of Keola's return.

They kissed their grandmother and started walking to the beach across the street. As they turned toward the house, they saw her waving to them. They waved back, high and tall, to the woman who had been their foundation and mother since they were infants.

Tutu felt tears fall down her cheek. One of them would die today. But even in the omen of the cloud was another large cloud looming over it. It was the cloud in the shape of a shark. This was the only thing that could save one of them from death. Only their shark god could save them.

Tutu walked into the house and went into the living room. She picked up her glasses and picked up the telephone. She dialed the numbers carefully and from memory. The phone rang four times before a male voice answered.

"Hi, Kawika. This is Aunty. I need you to come over right, right away," her voice pleaded into the telephone.

Kawika promised to be right over.

Next, Tutu called the one person whose strength and guidance she would need the most. She picked up the receiver and dialed her cousin, Laka.

The phone rang and rang and rang. There was no answer. Perhaps none of Laka's attendants were at home. She slumped over in her chair and allowed the phone to keep ringing. Each ring brought her closer to desperation.

Regarding the Children's Great Love
for Each Other

KEOLA AND PUA ENJOYED THE COOL OCEAN WATER. They dunked their entire bodies so that the water came up to their noses and they blew bubbles. The sight of each other blowing bubbles like when they were children made them laugh. Pua stood up in the ocean and held her round belly. "Stop before I give birth right now," she laughed.

Keola touched her stomach. "Is there really no hope for you and Tiki? What happened?" he asked.

"No. There is no hope for us. I did not tell him yet that I was pregnant. I do not know if he knows. I have not seen him for months." Pua looked at her cousin. "He hit me. He got angry one day and smashed a bucket into my face."

"He hit you?" Keola asked incredulously. "I can't believe it. He was so in love with you. Why didn't you tell me?"

"Tiki has his issues with his parents and that is something that he needs to deal with. I was a victim of that rage and I realized that until he worked it out with someone professional or even his parents, that anger would always be there, festering and incubating." Pua brushed her left palm against the face of the water. For a moment she stared at the scar where her finger had been. "Tutu taught us that. But I couldn't tell you because you were in training and I didn't want you to worry. Besides, I handled it myself."

Keola looked at his cousin and had never been more proud of her. "That must have been hard for you." Keola grabbed a handful of wet sand and let it run from one hand into the other. "He just left and didn't come back?"

Pua immersed herself up to her neck in the ocean. "He tried to get back together for a few months," she stammered. "It was hard but I knew that the rage was stronger than him." She exhaled a deep breath. "So much so that he doesn't even know that it is there. I couldn't put my baby or myself in that kind of danger. So I told him not to come around or I would tell everyone what had happened. I knew that would work because I knew that he didn't want to do anything that made Mr. and Mrs. Helekunihi ashamed of him."

"Whew. A lot of things happened while I was gone, cousin," Keola laughed.

"I couldn't tell Tutu what was going on. It would have worried her and it was too much for me to go over, you know?" Pua gathered her hair and squeezed the water out of it.

"I know the feeling. Kumu is the most intense teacher I have ever met and I cannot even begin to tell you the things that I see now. The nature of man is incredible and there is a whole level of healing that he will open your mind to. I cannot even begin to tell you the things that I am aware of now." Keola felt something squishy under his feet and looked down to see thousands of black sea cucumber. "Ha ha ha ha! Look at all of these!"

"Eww! I'm getting out of this water," Pua screamed.

Keola quickly picked up a sea cucumber, aimed its mouth at Pua, and squeezed the milky white fluid out. It shot her on the side of the head. She yelped.

Pua picked up two sea cucumbers, one in each hand, and squeezed them out at Keola. A stream of white hit him on his chest and in his hair. "Take that!" Pua screamed in joy.

"Pua, that's so disgusting!" Keola yelled at her.

"You started it!" She threw the sea cucumbers back into the water and ran for shore before Keola could exact his revenge on her again.

Keola immersed his entire body under the water and washed his hair, face, and chest of all the sticky white. He immersed himself twice to make sure that all the gunk was off of him, then he ran and plopped himself on the shore at Pua's feet. They were both laughing. They laughed so hard that they couldn't stop.

Then Pua felt her baby kick. It knocked the breath right out of her. She choked on her laugh.

"Pua, are you okay?" Keola moved toward her.

"The baby kicked!" Pua grabbed Keola's hand and placed it on her stomach.

It kicked again and Keola laughed. "I felt it! I felt it!"

The two cousins sat on the sand and relished this moment. It was one of the most precious days in their lives and they knew it.

All the laughter made them hungry and they unpacked the loaf of bread they had brought with the can of pork and beans. They opened the can and slathered the orange sauce over their slices of bread. They took out the jar of mayonnaise and coated a thick portion on their bread. They looked at each other and took huge bites, letting all the juice from the sandwiches drip onto their chins and into the sand.

"Hey, I haven't seen Kaleihepule," Keola commented. "Have you seen her?"

Pua looked to the horizon. "I haven't seen her for a while. She must be with Uncle Kawika or something. Sometimes she is here and sometimes she is not." Pua scanned the ocean. "I don't want to call her, though. No need for that."

"Yes. No need for that," Keola agreed and took another huge bite of his sandwich.

They both looked out to the horizon and let the sound of the gentle surf carry their thoughts out to the ocean.

TIKI STOOD BEHIND THE TREE and watched. The words in his mother's letter were true. His grandmother had seen the image of a child. Pua was pregnant.

The bloodlines of the shark and the centipede were intertwined.

He stared at Pua and Keola playing in the water and watched with jealousy as they laughed and laughed and laughed. When they began eating, he grew even angrier as he saw Keola reach over and feel Pua's stomach. By the way they were both behaving, he knew that the baby, his baby, was kicking.

He was at a crossroads. In his guts, with every bone and muscle in his body, he wanted to go over to Pua and proclaim his love for her and their child. But the prophecy held him back. His mother had chosen to recall it in her letter to him right before she died. It was killing him. He didn't know what to do.

One moment he was calm and collected. His thoughts were as clear and calm as the Waialua River. Then, the very next moment brought rage. How dare Pua not tell him that she was carrying their child? Why had she not called him? Would she dare allow Tiki to live his life and not know anything about the existence of a child? What kind of sick and hateful woman was she?

Tiki tried to control his anger. He spied on them from behind the tree for three hours while they enjoyed their lunch and swim.

TIKI ADMITTED TO HIMSELF that he was a mess. The last time he had felt this confused and angry, he had lost the most cherished thing in his life by hitting her with a bucket. He did not, could not, go to that dark place again. He decided to go back home and think about things.

When I am calm, I will go and talk to her, Tiki said to himself. She will understand that I have been trying to make something out of my life. She will see that I am a different person from the one who lost control and hit her on the head. Yes, she will see.

But as he turned around to leave, a rage swept over him. It was like a demon had possessed him and he sprinted over to Pua and Keola.

Pua pulled herself backward in shock. Keola stood up quickly.

"What do you want? Why are you here?" Pua yelled.

"Go home, Tiki!" Keola looked Tiki directly in the eyes. "I am telling you nicely. Just go home."

Tiki was so angry that he started to foam at the mouth. "Why didn't you tell me you were pregnant?" His eyes turned red with anger. "I have spent the last months making something of myself—going to school and working—so that I could make you a good husband. You weren't even honest with me. You didn't even respect me enough to tell me that you were carrying my baby," he screamed at her.

Pua feared for her life. Her baby started to kick and her belly started to move. "Tiki, stop! I don't feel well. Let's talk about this later."

"No!" Tiki stepped menacingly toward Pua. "We'll talk about it now!"

Keola grabbed Pua's hand and gently pulled her toward him. "Don't do anything you'll regret. Just go home and we'll talk about this with the family. All of us—even the Helekunihis." Keola tried to use a soothing voice to calm him down.

"You want to embarrass me in front of my foster parents? First you try to take away my baby and now you want to embarrass me in front of my foster parents? What did I ever do to you? Why are you so heartless?" He was shaking in rage.

"Tiki, we need to talk with all the family and make some choices. But we are not going to get anywhere unless you calm down. You are scaring Pua." Keola still used his soothing voice. "Let's all go back to the house and talk."

Pua's body started to ache. Her legs started to cramp and she felt a sensation of tightening under the baby. "Tiki, let me go home," she pleaded.

"Enough! We are leaving! Come over to the house when you are calm. Bring your foster parents and we will talk." Keola picked up their belongings, took Pua's arm, and started to walk away.

Tiki looked as if he had calmed down. His eyes were still red. He was still shaking. But it was as if the cloud of calmness had once again taken control of his body. He watched Pua and Keola leave the beach area.

Pua and Keola were just about fifteen feet from the road when they turned and saw Tiki tearing after them.

"Quick! Hurry home." Keola let go of Pua's arm. "I will stall him."

Pua turned and ran. She was so afraid. She was frantic. And she was so startled that she did not look before she ran into the street. When she looked to the left, the last thing she saw was the frightened, pitiful eyes of Lovey Helekunihi. Lovey's green Nova hit Pua on the left side and propelled her into a tall wooden telephone pole. Pua's entire body slammed into the pole, then slid down in what seemed like slow motion.

Lovey slammed on the brakes.

Tiki stopped dead in his tracks.

Only Keola, who had his back turned to Pua, did not see what happened. But he had heard the sound of Pua's body being hit by the car. And he had heard the sound of the brakes screeching.

Keola turned and looked for his cousin. He ran into the street and searched for his cousin in the direction of their house. She was not there. He turned slowly and saw her limp body lying at the base of the telephone pole. "No!"

Keola ran to her body and picked her up. "Pua! Pua!" He shook her. "Get up, cousin! Get up, cousin!" He felt something warm down his leg. His swim shorts were covered in blood. "No! Please!"

Tiki ran over to Pua and Keola. But when he neared, Keola growled at him like a ferocious wild pig protecting its young. He turned and went to the car to check on Lovey.

Lovey was stuck in the middle of the road. She had not moved. The car was still running. She was breathing heavily and staring out of the windshield. Tiki went to the side of the car and knocked on the glass.

When she didn't move, he opened the door. Lovey did not seem to have any cuts or bruises, but she was in complete shock.

"Open the back door, Tiki," Keola yelled. "Open the back door and drive us back to Tutu's house." Keola lifted Pua's body and got into the car. "Hurry! Drive us to Tutu's house! Now! Move! Now!"

Tiki shoved Lovey from the driver's seat into the passenger's seat. He shifted the car into drive and sped toward Tutu's house.

It seemed like forever but, finally, Tiki turned left into the lane by Tutu's house. As soon as he pulled into the dirt driveway, Tutu and Kawika came running outside.

Tutu put her hand on the large gash in Pua's side to stop the bleeding while Keola and Kawika carried her into the house. They laid her on the bed.

The noise of a car in the driveway startled everyone in the house.

"Keola! Come get me!" It was Laka. "Hurry!"

Keola ran outside to get his teacher.

"My nephew will take me inside. Thank you so much for driving me all this way. I am in your debt," Laka thanked his neighbor. "Take me quickly into the house. Tell Kawika to call all our family gods."

The Leaping Spirits of Kaena

KEOLA PLACED KUMU NEAR PUA'S HEAD. She was lying on the living room floor. Blood had started to pool at her torso.

Tutu removed Pua's clothes so that she could see if there were any more wounds. She checked for a heartbeat but there was none. She tried to force air into Pua's mouth but it was no use.

Pua was dead.

Her baby was dead.

Tutu turned toward Keola. "Put Lovey and Tiki in the car and send them home. Now." Tutu turned toward Kawika. "Go fetch some awa from the yard. Bring a gourd, and then call our god."

Keola did as he was told. He escorted Lovey outside and into the car. He turned toward Tiki. "We will call you as soon as there is news. Go home and take care of Mrs. Helekunihi."

Tiki obeyed Keola and started the car. Keola watched as the car exited the driveway and then the lane. He ran toward the backyard so that he could help Kawika prepare the awa.

Once the awa was pulverized, strained, and mixed with water, they took it back into the house. They offered it to Tutu and she held the awa up to Kumu's mouth. He closed his eyes and drank the entire contents of the cup. "Laka, go get her spirit back. When you have her spirit, wink, and we will plug the stopper into the gourd."

Laka let the awa take effect. Soon, his body felt relaxed. He felt something nudge his right side. It was Uluhala.

Laka felt his soul leave his body. His spirit form climbed onto Uluhala's back and they traveled westward toward the setting sun. His spirit flew over the temple of Kapukapuakea and Kaiaka. His spirit flew over Puuiki and Mokuleia. Soon, he could see spirits lined across the spirit-jumping cliffs of Leinakauhane, a cliff of Kaena.

Hundreds of spirits were waiting for the last portal of the day to jump off the cliff, the last frontier of the physical world, into the spirit world. They were waiting for the sun to set. They needed the last portal to open and that would only happen once the sun was positioned at the halawai, the horizon and meeting place of the land and the ocean.

There were so many spirits. Laka did not think that he had enough time to find the spirit of Pua among all of these other spirits. He was worried that the spirit of Pua and her infant would jump into the sun portal before he could find them. Once they disappeared into the spirit world, there would be no hope. They would be gone forever.

Laka chanted to the sun:

E Kanehoalani,
Greetings!
Throngs await your glory,
Waialua bows to your brilliance.
To Kane who lights up the heavens
caught by the sennit of a child of a bark cloth beater.
Please grant the request.
Stay, but a moment longer.
It is but a servant's request.

The sun granted his request. It stopped and allowed Laka to look for Pua and her child. Laka called out to the mass of souls who were on the cliff and poised to jump:

A child of Paalaa,
a pet of Lei.
I call to you.
Where are you?
I am the teacher of your beloved, Keola.

Life to you!
Here I am, Laka

Laka cocked his head to one side so that it was turned in the direction of the cliffs. On the other side, the ocean was roaring, but he tuned it out and listened intently.

From the far side of the cliff, he heard a female's voice:

Who calls to me?
I search the breadfruit of Leleiwi

Laka listened carefully and urged Uluhala to fly rapidly to the source of the voice. It was as she uttered her last words that Laka and Uluhala spotted her on the edge of the cliff. Her stomach was full with child.

They swept down. Although Laka did not have arms in the physical realm, he had them in the spiritual realm. With both fists, he grabbed Pua's spirit. She shrieked and tried to break free but he kept a tight grip on her. As soon as he had her on the back of Uluhala, they flew home.

Uluhala and Laka flew into the house and, seeing the gourd, they dropped Pua's soul into the empty container.

Laka clenched his eyes to signal Tutu that he had deposited Pua's spirit into the container. Tutu saw the signal and plugged the container shut with ti leaf and breadfruit sap.

Uluhala flew near Laka's face and Laka jumped off. His spirit form climbed into his tear ducts and back into his body. He awoke himself from his awa-induced stupor.

Laka looked at Keola. "Your Tutu and I will try to revive her. The ceremonies that we use must be free of fault. The first thing that you must do is gather important plants from the forest. We will need enough lehua to make twelve ropes. Then you must go even higher into the forest and obtain enough maile to make four ropes. Go!" Keola left and headed for the Koolau forest.

Laka turned toward Kawika. "Kawika, you must go to the beach and gather enough morning glory vines to braid into four ropes. Once you have gathered enough vines, you must gather water that has collected in the tops of the apu taro. This water is the purest form because it has not touched the ground. If there is not enough water in the tops of these plants around here, then you must climb into the water belt of the forest and collect the rainwater in your palms and place it in this gourd that has been purified. Fail in any of your tasks and Pua and her child will be lost forever to the spirit realm."

Laka watched as Tutu brought some fresh bark cloth. He watched as she lovingly cleaned the blood that had matted on Pua's hair and drenched her clothing.

Tutu did not shed a tear. Her resolve was so strong and her knowledge of healing equally so that she feared nothing. "How did you know to come, cousin?"

"The clouds."

"This will be hard on us. I am not a young girl anymore. I do not know if I can last for twenty days while we push her spirit back into her body." Tutu continued to wipe the blood from Pua's body.

"We have Keola and Kawika. Kawika is in charge of the family gods. And Keola has a gift that I have never seen before."

"This is why I sent him to you." Tutu wrung the cloth into a bowl. The water turned a bright red from the blood.

"We must teach him our way of healing," Laka added. "Our rituals are our own."

After Tutu had cleaned Pua's body, Tutu moved Pua so that her head was at the door. Pua's head was to the east and her feet were pointed to the west. This was a very important part of the revivification. The living room floor was going to be constructed like the globe, exactly as heiau are representations of the world. Pua's body would be symbolically placed on the equator. There would be twelve ropes of lehua that would represent the goddess Laka. Laka is condensation, precipitation, and evaporation. Man is mostly water.

The maile, a body form of the god Kane, would be placed in the realm that belonged to Kane, an area that began from the equator and went to the northernmost path of the sun's journey across the heavens, the Polohiwa a Kane.

The morning glory, a medicinal plant and a body form of the god Kanaloa, would be placed in the realm that belonged to Kanaloa. It was the area that began from the equator and extended to the southernmost path of the sun's travel from east to west, the Polohiwa a Kanaloa.

When the sun travels along the Polohiwa a Kane, it is the summer solstice. When the sun travels along the Polohiwa a Kanaloa, it is the winter solstice. When the sun travels along the middle of those heiau, it is either the fall equinox or the spring equinox. The heiau are aligned to the sun's path.

Kane is also the god of the east. His realm begins at sunrise and ends when the sun is directly overhead, when the sun casts no shadow. Once the sun begins its descent, then that is the realm of Kanaloa.

This is the universe that Laka and Tutu were creating with the lei. They were going to build the universe according to the sun's path. They were also using the medicinal and symbolic meanings of the maile, lehua, and morning glory to revive Pua.

Once Pua's body was cleaned, Tutu purified the body to make it a proper vessel to receive the spirit. "If we are to do this correctly, we will need the help of everyone—including the gods. If it were one person it would be easier, but I have never revived an unborn dead child before." Tutu looked lovingly at her granddaughter.

"The child will make it harder because it has not yet learned to love this life," Laka admitted. "We must rely on the love of the mother to call out to her child so that its spirit comes as well."

Tutu walked over to her cousin. "I will take the first watch over my granddaughter. Let me carry you into the bedroom so that you can rest. The day will be a long one."

Laka let himself be carried by Tutu. She was still a strong woman and she carried him with ease. She took him to the bathroom so that he could take care of his needs and then she put him to bed.

Tutu returned to the living room, took a seat over the body of her granddaughter, and planned out the following day.

LAKA AWOKE EARLY IN THE MORNING to the sound of footsteps in the hall. His keen sense of hearing told him that it was Keola. "Are you back already?" he asked.

"Yes. Kawika and I returned a short time ago. Everything is ready for you." Keola came into the bedroom and picked up his teacher.

"You are the one who will be conducting today's healing ceremonies," Laka revealed to Keola. "Today you will become a healer."

Keola was stunned. "I cannot take this responsibility. It is too much for me. I am not focused and I might make a mistake."

"What better person is there? You love her more than you love yourself. Your prayers will be deliberate and perfect," Laka said in a serious tone. "Take me to wash up."

Keola took his teacher into the bathroom to wash up. When Kumu was done, they entered the living room where Tutu and Kawika were braiding the plants.

Laka commanded them to arrange the plants in a specific order: "In order to force the spirit back into this body, we will need to call upon some of these gods for their help. The first gods that we will call upon are Laka, Kane, and Kanaloa, for those are the gods of life and death, and the gods of the water, the waters of life, the surface waters, and the still, deep waters of the underground aquifers."

Keola and Kawika took the lei and made sure that they were perfectly made. Each lei was braided so that it was thick and looked like an umbilical cord.

"This ceremony will have three parts. The first part will be to prepare the body for the spirit because it is a vessel that will need to be purified. The second will be to offer the various chants to call for the spirit and command it to enter the body. Once the spirit has entered the body, the third part will be to rub the entire body with oil as a final preparation and protection." Laka looked at Kawika and Keola. "Kawika, I will need you to call forth our gods. They will be the haka between this world that we live in and the godly realm. We will rely on them to communicate our prayers and wishes to the various gods."

"Yes," Kawika responded.

"Keola, as I have said before, you will conduct the ceremonies and offer the chants. Do not be concerned if there are words coming out of your mouth that you do not understand. It is only our gods who are giving you the words. Trust in your connection with them and they will not fail you."

"Yes, Kumu," Keola said with resolve.

"Good. Take the lei of lehua and arrange them on the living room floor like this: there should be four strands of lehua. Two parallel strands running east to west that begin at the door and end where we will place Pua's navel, and two that begin at her navel and end at her feet. These lei will represent the sun traveling at the midpoint, the equinox, when the length of the day is equal to the length of the night." Laka supervised the construction of the lei.

When the lei were braided to his liking, Laka said, "The sun is life. We will harness the four corners in order to pull all of the mana from the universe. Man is a part of the universe and the universe is a part of man. This is the only way we can get enough strength to place her spirit back into her body."

Gingerly, they placed Pua's body on the lei of lehua. Her head was near the door and on an east-west alignment.

Laka directed Kawika and Keola on how to place the lei. "We will connect eight lei to Pua's navel and to the eight cardinal and intercardinal points. This will give the impression of an octopus lying on the stomach of Pua. This octopus will pull the sickness out of her body and disperse it while at the same time pull the energy from the universe and push it into her navel. We thank the god Kanaloa for this action, this pathway that facilitates this transfer of energy. It is true, dear family, that Hiiakaikapoliopele did utilize the same methods while healing the husband, Lohiauipo." He continued, "Pua has been placed on four lei of lehua. We will take the maile and construct the north quadrant of the heiau because the maile is a form of the god Kane and it is he who controls that realm. Then we will take the morning glory vines and construct the southern quadrant of the heiau because that realm belongs to Kanaloa." Laka surveyed the rectangle perimeter of lei that enclosed Pua's body.

He continued, "Take the remaining lehua and lay one end to her navel and the other end to the Kai Koolau. Place lei connecting each cardinal point and intercardinal point. There will be eight lei. Go all the way until you are lining up lei with her navel and the Kai Puna and then continue until you have used all eight lei."

Kawika thought that Pua looked like a navigation compass. After he was done helping Keola lay the lei, he waited patiently until Laka gave him further directions.

In total, there were four maile lei, four lei of morning glory vine, and twelve lei of lehua.

Everything looked perfect to Laka. "Now we will begin the prayers. This will take twenty days to complete. We will pray for her for twenty days. Remember that any fault in the protocol will mean that Pua will die."

Tutu Recalls the Revivification of Kawanana

OUR FAMILY HAS DONE THIS BEFORE, Keola. We have brought someone back from death. And two things happen when you bring someone back from death.

The first thing is that you realize that your perceptions of life on this earth change. You are at the height of your abilities. You are now responsible for this awesome power. The gods are on your side and you feel indestructible. You become more patient. You don't stress about any old thing because everything is little compared to death.

The second thing is that when you enter into the spirit world, when you touch a dead body and help her come back to life, you go to another realm. The daily living of life becomes mundane. This is a gift. It is a gift to be in touch with the spirits and the other realm. But you cannot stay there. You must come back. This is the place for the living. And anytime the spirit world communicates with you, you have to think deeply about what they are saying to you. Sometimes the visions and messages that we get can be harmful so we must break them as soon as they come to us. We must say, "I break this." Or, "Return this evil to the person who sent it to me." This is how we take care of those things.

I tell you this now because after this, your life will change. If you are succesful, then you will know things that very few people know. But if you fail, you will think that you are not worthy. If you allow this feeling to take root in your personality, it will never let go and it will drive you crazy.

Focus on what is supposed to be and let that be the answer. Do not think of yourself as the answer. Think of yourself only as the conduit.

FOR MONTHS, A MAN NAMED FORBES PESTERED my grandfather. He claimed that he did research.

He wanted to talk to my Tutu because my Tutu was responsible for caring for burial caves. These caves were where chiefs were taken when they died. My grandfather took care of them. He watched over them. He was the only one in the village that was trusted enough to know where all the burials were. And he took this responsibility very seriously.

Every day, the Forbes man came to my grandfather and tried to talk to him. But my grandfather didn't want to have anything to do with this man. Later, he would say that he just got a bad feeling from him.

Anyway, Forbes came every day to talk to my grandfather. He always wanted to know where the caves were. But my grandfather told him that he had no reason for going there.

But this man was persistent. My grandfather was patient and was loving so he tolerated Forbes but under no circumstances would he reveal anything about the caves.

But Forbes found out where the caves were. He took some other men and they looted all the caves! They took all of the funerary objects that had been buried with the chiefs: the images, the gods, the bark cloth, everything. They had even been so disrespectful as to use one of the skulls as a candleholder—can you imagine? They took one of the chief's skulls and stuck a candle on it so there was light enough for them to see all the things to steal.

My grandfather ran up to the caves as fast as his feet could carry him. And when he got to the caves he saw that the worst possible thing that he imagined had happened. Forbes had taken all the personal items of the dead. He had taken the skeletons. He had taken the wooden gods. Everything was gone.

My grandfather was utterly devastated.

We don't know how someone could take things from the dead and consider it research. All I know now is that wherever that man is, I hope he is treated the same way that he treated the chiefs that day.

My grandfather climbed down from the mountain. He did not go home. He did not even go back to the village. He went back to the beach and got in his canoe and he paddled out. He traveled so far out that you could not even see him anymore. And he stayed in his canoe and drifted.

He did not eat. He did not drink. He wanted to die. He felt so guilty for having betrayed the trust of the chiefs.

But it wasn't him. My grandfather did not ever reveal to Forbes where the caves were. Later, they found out that it was his brother who sold out the chiefs for a few dollars. But my grandfather felt responsible.

My grandfather felt so guilty that he sailed into the ocean and expected to die there. He punished himself first before dying.

He was out on that canoe for a long time. We do not know how long he had been dead. Many say he died from starvation and thirst. But my grandmother says he died of a broken heart.

Kaleihepule flipped the canoe over and brought him to the shore where Grandmother found him. The family built a house made out of ti leaf on the beach and for almost a month we did the rituals to bring him back to life.

Keola, what will be, will be. We are only servants of the gods who have a bigger plan. Our duty is to only take care of what we have until the next generation. We have done this before. Have faith. Let your love for your cousin be your guide but don't let it distract you.

Let's begin.

The Healers

KEOLA BEGAN THE FIRST CHANT and did not stop until he was done. At the end of the first chant, he looked at his grandmother and then at Laka. "Tutu. How was my chant?" Keola asked Tutu.

"There was no mistake from the time you uttered the first word until the time you uttered the last word. Perhaps the only fault is that you rushed the chant and it ended sooner than it should have."

Keola replied, "Yes, that is possible as I want my cousin to come back already." He sighed. "But speed is not an issue here. The words are the most important." And then with the determination of the surf, he started his second chant.

His goal in this chant was to evoke the names of the powerful gods to aid him in his quest to revive his cousin and beloved. Among the names that he evoked were the deities from the Time-before-the-Great-Landing. These gods came over the Pacific with the first navigators.

He gave five chants in perfect pitch and pace. These chants were from an established protocol and hierarchy. In addition, after each chant he asked his grandmother and teacher if they found fault with anything that he said. Each time they responded that indeed, his chant had been perfect.

The final chant called upon the tumultuous, primal nature of the world when all the elements—wind, fire, thunder, lightning, and earth—function as one chaotic mass. He noted that when the volcano erupts it spouts hot lava and gasses into the air that stirs the clouds to create thunder and lightning that hits the earth. This plume of smoke, ash, rain, lava, and lightning has been described in chants. Keola alluded to them now in both honor and awe of the fantastic forces of nature. Man's return from the dead was an unnatural act. Only the elements could agree to this. Only lightning, such as in the possession of the god Kauilanuima-kaehaikalani, could act as a defibrillator and rejuvenate Pua's body with a jolt of energy sufficient to revive her.

The words and the poetry of the chants were the offering. The sincerity of his chant was the offering. The resolve of attaining his most ardent wish was the offering.

AFTER CHANTING THE FIVE SEPARATE PRAYERS, Keola looked up and was glad to see Tutu smiling at him. "We are done for today." She touched his cheek. "Tomorrow we begin again." The others went into the kitchen to eat steamed taro tops. There would be no meat served until Pua was back in her body or until she died.

Tonight, Kawika watched over the body of Pua. He sipped awa and spoke to Pua. He explained everything. He even explained how Keola had risen to the occasion in order to get her soul placed back in her body.

"I am worried for her child," Tutu said. "I can feel his fascination for the spirit world because it is the only thing that he knows."

Kawika used the most reassuring tone in his voice that he could muster. "Do not worry. When the time comes and your body is ready to accept you again, we will all help, even the ancestors."

"Yes, we need them now." Tutu placed her hand on Kawika's shoulder. "We need them more than we ever have."

Tutu Talks about the Death of Kawanana

If There Is No Hope, There Is No Cure

PINEA AND KEALO HAD SEARCHED EVERYWHERE for their husband. They searched his favorite hunting spots, but he was not there. Besides, he would not have gone hunting without his favorite spear. They searched his favorite fishing spots, but he was not there. Besides, he would not have gone fishing without his favorite lures. They searched all the neighboring villages but no one had seen him.

One of the village children had been looking for crabs when Kaleihepule was seen with the limp Kawanana on her back. The child ran so fast that he could not even speak by the time that he got to Pinea and Kealo. But they knew that it was something important and concerning Kawanana so they told the child to show them where he was. The entire village overheard the panic in this child's voice as he tried to explain what he had seen at the beach. They followed him to Kawanana.

Kealo and Pinea recognized him from a distance. This was the man with whom they had shared their house and their lives. They knew every curve of his body and every hair on his head. This was the man the sisters loved as equally as they loved each other. It was their core that recognized this man before their eyes did. Their eyes would only confirm this. But, in their very core, they also knew that he was dead.

Pinea and Kealo dragged Kawanana onto the shore. His mouth had no breath. His heart had no beat. His eyes had no reflection.

The sisters did not talk. They had a singular purpose. They would try to bring their husband back to the realm of the living. They turned toward the people who had followed them to the beach and gave directions on how to acquire everything they needed for their ceremony.

Kalau was responsible for obtaining all the greenery from the forests. I was responsible for building and keeping the fire. Hanalei was responsible for gathering the fresh and the salt water for the ceremony. Laka was the medium that would bridge the gap between our world and the spirit world. At that time, he was the youngest haka ever.

Laka drank awa, and ascended into the spirit realm. He hopped on the back of Uluhala and began searching. In her lifetime, Uluhala had been a renowned healer. Our knowledge comes from her. When she died, she was turned into a family guardian. Her spirit chose the form of a bat and that was the form that she used when we called upon her to help us. Laka tried to find his grandpa's spirit.

Laka found Grandpa's spirit at the banks of Ukoa fishpond. His spirit had just fished out one of the mysterious fishes of that special fishpond in Haleiwa. People from our area knew that the fishes in that pond were special. The fish in that pond were half a variety of one fish and half the variety of another at the same time.

When Laka looked at the fish, he made a mental note that one side of the fish was a striped mullet and the other side of the fish was a milkfish. This omen did not go unnoticed by Laka. There was an equal chance of death and an equal chance of life.

Laka enticed Kawanana's spirit with a candlenut that had been lit at the end of a palm frond. The nut only had enough oil to stay lit for three minutes so Laka knew that he had to hurry. He waved the light in front of Kawanana's face and spoke softly to the spirit to follow him.

The light attracted Kawanana. And my grandfather started to follow it.

LAKA LED MY GRANDFATHER'S spirit to the ti-leaf house that had been built at the shore. The house faced the east. The rising sun would touch the body of Kawanana every day until the rite was completed.

During the time that my grandmother and her sister used their skills to bring my grandfather back to life, the entire village tried their best to help in any way that they could. They killed all of the chickens and silenced the dogs and the pet pigs by tying their mouths shut with rope. The village did their best to keep the taboo of silence. The people of the village provided Pinea and Kealo with all of the special plants and fish and greenery that they needed.

The entire village really loved my grandfather because he was cut from the old cloth. He was kind. He was considerate. He could fix anything. And, most of all, he loved our people. Out of all the people in the village, who could have been entrusted with caring for those caves that contained the bones and afterlife objects?

A dead person was defiled. As soon as anything came into contact with a dead body, that object, too, was defiled. We would never consider going up to these caves and robbing them. But this man had done that. He stole defiled things from their graves.

My family, I will tell you a secret that I have held onto for over fifty, maybe sixty, years. I believed that my grandfather did the right thing by killing himself. I never told my family—not even Uncle Hanalei—how I ever felt. But I believe that Kawanana did not protect those bones as well as he should have. We later heard that the things they found in the cave had been sold, but we could not prove it. The entire village was devastated and we still carry the shame of that with us. I have secretly wanted to make a curse to give the thief a slow and painful death, but where do I send it? The dead depend on us to protect them and the things they need with them for the next life. If we cannot offer them that, then we are not a people of substance.

MY GRANDMOTHER AND HER SISTER PRAYED and massaged and chanted. They called forth all of the gods in the Hawaiian world to come and help them. But in the end, my grandfather was not allowed to return. Then, Pinea and Kealo tried to make Kawanana into a god. It did not work. His soul refused to enter into any animal form. It was snatched by a moth and taken into the Realm of Milu where it still resides to this day.

If you ask any of our family, they will say that it was because he was dead too long and it is impossible for anyone to return after that extended period of time in the realm of the dead. If you ask me, I will say that maybe the dead did not think that he deserved to return. In any event, he did not come back.

I still use that memory when I heal. It reminds me that people can be filled with hope and love. But they can also be filled with rage. If there is rage, it will consume everything. If there is rage, there is no hope and no cure.

Ceremony of Water

THE CEREMONY OF WATER BEGAN THE NEXT NIGHT. As instructed, Kawika and Keola had ventured out and collected water captured in the leaves of taro and rain.

Tutu put water in a gourd and put it near Pua's feet. She took another gourd and placed it near Pua's head. She took a third gourd, a water gourd with a thin neck, and placed it near Pua's navel.

"The braided lehua is an umbilical cord. The only water more pure than the water you have collected is the placenta—the birth waters. In order for this rebirth to happen, we must be sure that the body is pure." Laka looked at Keola. "You will do a chant to praise the living waters of Kane. If more of the lehua lei jumps into the gourd near you, then your prayers have been successful and Pua will live." He looked toward Kawika, who sat at Pua's feet. "If more lehua lei jump into your gourd, then the gods have rebuked Keola's attempts and Pua and her child will die. She will begin to smell and we shall have to bury her in the sand dunes of Kawailoa."

Keola chanted to Kaneikawaiola and to Lononuinohoikawai. As soon as his chant was finished, the lehua lei pulled away from their cardinal and intercardinal points and jumped into either gourd of water.

"How many lei are in your gourd, Kawika?" Tutu asked.

"How many lei are in your gourd, Keola?" Laka asked.

Both men held up their fingers. Keola had more lei in his gourd. Carefully, they returned the lei to the gourds.

"The gods have spoken. Pua will be healed," Laka exclaimed. "But Keola must do one more chant in order to release the evil that caused this body to eject its soul."

Keola took a deep breath and uttered a chant to release this evil. At the end of the prayer, he turned to Tutu and asked her, "How was my prayer, Tutu?"

"It was a good prayer. It was excellent, my darling," Tutu replied.

For three days, they presided over Pua's body. The power of their prayers and their purification ceremony preserved the body. Pua looked as if she were sleeping.

They offered prayers for the next four nights, in the moons known as the Ole moons. On the fifth night, before the moon called Huna rose, Laka asked Kawika to go to the ocean and get a variety of red fish. This would be the offering for the god Kauilanuimakaehaikalani. They hoped that the god would send lightning into Pua's body to revive her. Life was now closer to her than death.

When Kawika went to the ocean, he was not surprised to see that Kaleihepule had already anticipated the needs of the ceremony. Kaleihepule had corralled hundreds of red fishes.

As Kawika went into the water to take a closer look at the fishes, he noticed that Kaleihepule had amassed one type of fish, the red-and-white squirrelfish. "You are smarter than any one of us." Kawika smiled. He picked up one of the fish and threw it to Kaleihepule to eat. Then he got his fishing bag and held it open and his god chased the fish into the bag. When the bag was full, Kawika threw the bag onto the shore and swam a while with Kaleihepule. It felt so good to be in the water again. It felt good to be in the company of something that loved him completely.

When he was done swimming, Kawika climbed the sandy hill and went to Tutu's house. He walked into the house with the bag of fish and laid them out at Pua's feet.

Laka and Tutu noticed that there was only one variety of fish. "Kaleihepule knows well the evil that affects Pua." Laka smiled. "This is the fish that eats sea worms."

In one instant, the visions of the centipede and the warning of the muiona were revealed. Tiki had a centipede for an aumakua and it was trying to communicate with their family. If Tiki were really connected and paying attention, his family god would have cared for him. However, Tiki was lost.

Keola started to chant to the god to plant a spark of life into Pua and the baby she was carrying. As soon as he ended the last syllable of his chant, the fish vanished from the area around Pua's feet.

More days passed, each with its own set of prayers and rituals. "Tonight is the night that we will anoint Pua with oil," Laka directed. The entire family gathered around Pua and used coconut oil to anoint her body.

On the next night, Laka called the entire family to place themselves around a large bowl of awa that he had instructed Kawika to make. This was the night that the spirit of Pua and her child would reenter their vessels. They each drank several coconut bowls of awa.

As the awa opened the portal wide for his ancestors to emerge from the spirit realm, Laka asked Tutu to start.

Tutu removed the ti leaf, undid the breadfruit sap, and placed the opening of the container containing Pua's spirit at Pua's feet. Slowly she opened Pua's mouth and poured the spirit into it.

When the spirit was in the proper position, they started to massage the baby's spirit that had been left in Pua's solar plexus while they worked on his mother. They took the little spirit and pushed it through the umbilical cord. From the red cord to the tiny tips of his toes, the spiritual hands completed this work. They pressed, prodded, and cajoled the youngster into returning to his body.

Pua opened her eyes. She took in a deep breath.

She lay startled for the rest of the night and the next day. Her body had been inactive for so long that she could not get up. The family persisted in their love and faith for her recovery.

Soon, she was able to move a toe and then a finger. Then she could move her foot an inch and she could raise her hands off the floor.

When she was almost able to get up, Tutu took some water and sprinkled it on her eyes. Tutu took salt water and massaged her arms, her feet, and her belly.

Pua stood up, wobbly at first, then finally strong. She put her hand on her stomach and sensed that everything was fine with her child. She looked around and started to cry. The family gathered around her and showered her with kisses while Laka smiled.

All of a sudden, Pua grabbed her stomach and bent over in pain as the first contraction knocked her breath out of her body. Then she felt warm liquid run down her legs. Her water had broken.

"My son is coming." Her eyes were as round as breadfruit. "My son is coming."

About the Author

Kimo Armitage is an award-winning author who has published more than twenty books, mainly for children and young adults. Raised in Haleʻiwa by his maternal grandparents, he is instructional faculty at Kamakakūokalani—The Center for Hawaiian Studies at the University of Hawaiʻi at Mānoa where he teaches Hawaiian and Indigenous Literature.

About the Cover Artist

Maile Andrade is a multimedia visual artist and professor at Kamakakūokalani—The Center for Hawaiian Studies at the University of Hawaiʻi at Mānoa, developing and teaching in a Native Hawaiian creative expression program. She has exhibited her works locally, nationally, and internationally.